I Am Uncle Sam

Dean Mosley

This Book Is Dedicated To The Young Men Of The West, For Whom Heritage And Homeland Is Everything.

Chapter 1
New York, John F. Kennedy Airport
September 7 1966
|Augustus Doctor|

Three years ago I enlisted soon after my birthday to do what I could to protect this dear land from Soviet expansion; three years ago, the president promised our war would be defensive; three years ago, he was assassinated and his successor took seat. We have a new president now, not a man I can rightly say I ever respected, nor trusted.

I didn't like the old president either, wouldn't entrust him with the nation, nor its future. I'd have voted against him if I could at the time, but at least he was a run of the mill, slow-pace politician. I only saw him a temporary, harmless phase for the country, the new guy on the other hand; he had some more explosive rhetoric, and the new pace of the country began to worry me. I'd ended up in the wrong place at the wrong time you could say, 'fighting in a far off land while power exchanged hands so abruptly, but I accepted it; I've already lain my hand at the table, and if we were to go on the offensive instead of hold our ground, it wasn't my place to say otherwise.

Two years ago the new President reassured us that our job would keep a defensive character, that Vietnam would not become another Korea, but by the end of the year our men in Vietnam had doubled in number, and we'd started running a combination of land charges supplemented by bombing runs.

I tried to keep a close ear to the news back home, you get to miss it a lot when you're away. Like a lover, you hope she's safe, but start to worry when stories don't come back completely clear. This new President was telling our people the war effort was still defensive, while here in 'Nam we were instructed on precisely the contrary. Now, I understand it's a tough place to be in; between knowingly sending more after more upstanding, freedom-loving patriots to die, or the alternative, being to let the communists win, but ‘Nam isn't our home, ‘Nam doesn't affect us; I don't believe it ever has. This was an effort worth supporting, but not a war worth fighting. It probably came off that way to him, the president, at some point, but he decided to keep going.

We've lost this war, no matter how much of ‘Nam we hold. No foreign land is worth this much American blood. I'll have no more part in it.

I'm going home to protect my country where it counts, however that might be; but a lot can change in three years.
Three tours I've served, and the only one of my squad unit to make it through our last operation. ‘Told me I could go home with the next batch of soldiers if I was really done. They'd hoped to promote me to lead a small battalion, but I'll have no more patriots blood on my hands. It's a fools war we're fighting, and at this pace there'll be no patriots left to fight it. We'll be a nation of cowards ripe for Communist conquest.
Speak of the devil, a College-Type protest party was geared up to greet us at the airport with vicious, hate filled shouts; as if we were more monstrous to them than the Vietcong who were butchering our boys.

I hoisted my duffle bag off of baggage claim. It really upset me, for my efforts and the sacrifice of my team to be jeered as if I were the unwelcomed, but I wasn't about to encourage them, so I kept silent.

“-Didn't you hear me! Killers aren't welcome here! **You're not welcome here!**” I heard one yell close behind me. ‘*No, I heard you.*’ I thought to myself.

“Hey, shut your mouth, you damn beatnik!” A negro vet yelled back as he'd got to the bag-claim.

I turned to see the one who shouted at me, and a brood of four other liberal students who'd broken away from the bigger crowd, carrying with them sloppy anti-war signs, looking like something a kindergartener would make, albeit a vulgar one; they were following me.

"So this is our welcoming party, huh? You know, when my granddad got back from WW1 he got a parade." I said trying to dismiss myself without losing my temper, but they wouldn't have it; one of their women had grabbed onto my duffle bag, and tried pulling it away from me; I yanked it back, not meaning to pull that hard, but along she came, just catching herself from falling while the others hurried into a frenzy as if I'd attacked her. They started reaching for my bag and my pockets. Enraged, they started chanting all manner of obscenities at me while ***they*** attempted to rob ***me***.
"Get off of me, you dirty beatniks!" I shouted, slugging one of them in the face, and pulling my duffle away from the rest who just gawked at me in shock, as if I was in the wrong. I paced away, in awe myself of what had just happened.

"You fascist!" One of the girls yelled out to me as I walked off, readjusting the collar of my shirt and zipping my bag back up.

"These pinko college kids just get worse and worse." I thought.

I hate this damn city. Even before I left, I knew this place was no good: Crime, poverty, perversity, greed, all veiled by signs meant to distract, and bland towering metal buildings that blind you to the fact you're walking through extended gutters.

I had to collect my belongings: Cash, clothes, books. I have a friend up in New England who owns a little farm, 'told me he could provide me a job when I got back. First I'd have to make my way through the city, up from Brooklyn to Port Authority in Manhattan to take a transfer bus to a New England rail line.

I'd shuttled my way back to my old neighborhood in Brooklyn, a decent little space sequestered far enough from the city to keep the sewage from spreading, or so I thought. I stepped into my favorite little deli to buy myself a sandwich. Mr.Panucci was a first generation italian immigrant who opened this shop up when I was young. I remember coming in here after school on Fridays to grab a bite, but today Mr.Panucci was nowhere to be found, and the shop was uncomfortably cramped with tight shelves and unfamiliar product. I made my way back to where the deli used to be, only to find a Chinaman behind the counter.

The old menu still hung up behind him so I begrudgingly asked, "Excuse me, do you uh-. I wouldn't reckon you still serve sandwiches, now do you?"

"No sandwich. Old menu. Old menu." He repeated in broken english, gesturing to the sign. "You want buy something?" He asked while I glanced around.

"No thanks." I said turning around, accidentally knocking my duffle bag into a shelf, dropping and spilling four bottles of some black liquid I couldn't recognize. The man behind the counter shouted at me in a high pitch as they shattered.

"You pay! You pay for that!" He yelled as I tried to keep a distance from the shelves, but began unintentionally moving toward the door. "No! You pay! I call police!" He shouted.

"Easy pal, it was an accident. Give me a break." I said.

"You break, you pay!" He yelled.

"Look, I'll cover it, I-I'm sorry. How much is it? Five?"

"That thirty dollar!" He yelled.

"Thirty dollars for that? You're kidding, I only have twenty, I need to go to the bank!"

He didn't like the sound of that, and started cussing me out in Vietnamese. I slammed my hand on the counter. We began shouting at each other before he reached for the phone. I bolted out of that shop, knocking over another shelf of bottles on my way out; I didn't mean to, but I didn't care either.

"What the hell is wrong with this damn place!? I've been gone too long."

I had ducked away after running two blocks and an avenue. I felt like I was losing my mind. I just wanted to get away from this place. I withdrew my money from the bank, and cooled my temper, but upon stepping down into the subway station I found myself repulsed by the unkempt state of the damn place; it stank of urine, the walls and subway cars were defaced with graffiti, beggars lined the walls, rattling their mugs of change, and covertly injecting substance under cover of shadows while women and children walked by.

Most civilians just pretended they weren't there, but I stared right at these junkies with a glare. Some looked away in shame, one just grinned, the words "*Great Society*" were spraypainted behind him.

I'd be shut of it all, soon enough.

Times Square is my next stop. I have a storage locker that I need to gather a weeks worth of clothes from, and my book stack, both my reading material and journals, they helped me to compartmentalize my work, stay on top of things.

The subway crowd, still, left me feeling uneasy; across from me, I could hear a group of men speaking in Spanish, one holding an opened beer bottle, tipsily dripping its contents on the floor. To my left I saw a row of college-type beatniks with grotesquely dyed hair, their women shamelessly wearing close to nothing, outfits that left little to the imagination but sex. Yet to my right was a rather normal man just reading the paper as if nothing was wrong, the paper's

headline read "*Prez. To Assume Greater Jurisdiction To Ease Race Riots In Major Cities*";
I couldn't rush myself to the storage center quickly enough. Suffice to say, and I'll say it again, I was eager to be shut of New York.

I packed my duffle with my belongings, and took for Port Authority, when suddenly a tear in my duffle left by those beatniks gave way, spilling my things across the streets of Manhattan; passersby not even stopping to allow me a moment to gather my items together, but trampling and kicking them along, not even looking down. In a sea of people, my possessions drifted away, leaving me only the clothes on my back, my ID, and my bank money which I clutched tightly to ensure no one would seize that.

I had waited a bit for the crowd to thin so I could reclaim my possessions then, but even as it grew dark, the streets remained dense, eventually I gave up hope.

I retreated to the terminal, mounted a bus, and decided "*to hell with it*", I didn't care if this place robbed me; I didn't care that it'd become a total shithole, I just never wanted to see it again. The air-conditioned atmosphere of the bus felt a world cleaner than the thick, dirty feel of the subway air, and sweaty ambience of the crowded streets. I looked my ticket over to kill some time.
I felt an empty sadness inside of me; it felt like a foreboding worry, of some loss, but I reckoned I'd feel fine once I was accommodated far from this place.

The bus had come to a slow stop approximately ten, or maybe fifteen minutes in. The driver told us we'd be making an unexpected rest stop in Harlem. I looked out the window to see a crowd surrounding a church: White men in white shirts and khaki pants carrying signs, and a group of negroes in black suit jackets opposite them carrying their own signs. Protesters and counter protesters, it seemed, something to do with the riots probably.

I asked the bus driver how long we'd be delayed, he told me until the streets cleared, '*could be as much as an hour, might be more*. I got off with some other passengers who went to grab some food or use the restroom, I on the other hand wanted to see what the commotion was about.

The protesters were carrying signs which read things to the tune of "*Tyrant In Office*", "*America For Whites*", "*Africa For Africans*". As I walked around, it didn't seem like these two factions were against each other, but rather, protesting together.
Suddenly a voice came over a loudspeaker, a man at a podium holding a rolled up document in one hand, and gesturing with it.

"Gentlemen, we are now in the throws of a socio-political shift, one which will determine if this land will continue to be dominated by the good, moral, christian people who built it, or if it will be surrendered for domination to a bunch of beatnik scum, communists, illegals and all who would wish to take our land away from us. This past decade has laid bare for us to witness an accelerating change in the direction of our country from strength and tradition to liberal socialism, so much that it would seem the very moral compass of the nation has been hijacked and set a spin by nefarious agents! If you were to tell any American the truth of this trajectory, that in fifty years time, we whites will no longer be a majority in our own country, why no one would tolerate it, but at every attempt to bring up the truth, we're called hateful and racist, for what, for not wanting our country taken away from us!? The founders of this country had put together a very nice phrase in the declaration of independence, and it states '*whenever any form of government becomes destructive to the rights and securities of its public, it becomes the peoples duty to abolish it*'! Has this government become what our founders fought against? Will you, then, continue to obey this government soon to turn against us, or will we follow the laws instilled in us by our god and founders to protect and defend our liberties, the liberties of our children and our children's children? Now I look at you and I see a lot of young faces; when I was young, I'd been swindled into enlisting my life into the war against Japan and Germany, convinced by propaganda that they were the most vile and monstrous people on the planet, a message I and countless other American Christians bought into, and sacrificed for, while our government got itself cozy with the Soviets! Now they send our boys to Vietnam to die on the same alter, all in the name of containing communism, while the real communists are right here, infiltrating our government to promote socialism, liberalism, race-mixing, and debauchery! It's one big manipulation game; the Negro too being exploited as a weapon to shatter the American order in which his own race thrives, buying into the lies of equality and integration, while destroying the hegemony of white rule for white communities, and black rule for black communities. They shun our good men like Ford and McCarthy while pushing false saviors in the form of Goldwater and Martin Luther *Coon*. We have a tyrant in the white house, one who likely killed to get where he is, and doesn't seem to have any intention of leaving! Each year sees our homeland sink deeper and deeper into delusions of socialistic idealism, which you will pay the price for if we do not swiftly stop and reverse course. I say to you, gentlemen, that if you will stick together, that's the key, we can have our country once again free; we can have it once again ours; we can have a strong republic which every American can be proud of! Thank you all very much." He stepped down from his platform and began taking some questions for a number of journalists it would seem.

I made my way over to him, being blocked every few steps by someone checking me for weapons, until finally I was before him. I wanted to learn more. I extended my hand, he smiled and shook it.

"I'm Augustus Doctor-" I said. "-what you said up there really hit close to home for me, more than you might imagine, yet I'm afraid to say I don't even know who you are-" I paused, recalling he mentioned his time in the military, and thus I punctuated my question appropriately "-sir."
He seemed to appreciate this.

"You can call me Commander, son. How can I help you?"

London, Imperial War Museum
October 8 1966
|Garrath King|

"Artillery piece; World War Two; German. So strange to be this close to one." My father said to me as he laid his hand to the fifteen foot tall cannon. "I'd seen them during the war, but seeing one up close is far different from flying over, isn't it?" I looked around at the other exhibits as father continued. "Yes sir, 'tis a right honorable cache of memorabilia."

Father knelt down as he was a tall man, and though I was a boy of fifteen, he still towered over me and often over any another man in the room. "See, son, museums aren't just vessels for us to preserve our history-" He knelt forward, grinning. "-they're trophy rooms! Everyone of these halls dedicated to a great war we or our good men in the commonwealth fought, and most often, won. A testament to English achievement and capability, boy."

He placed his hand on my shoulder. "So that we never forget what we're capable of, what we fought for, and most importantly, who we are." He stood up and let out a heavy dry cough. "Best we start wrapping up this tour I suppose. I should've dressed more appropriately for the season, but October's never felt this cold before."

"You can head home, dad, I just want to browse the collections a bit longer."

"Now lad, you do know your way home, right-now?"

"Yes sir, the tram should take me a few blocks away. I could even make my way on foot if I had to."

"Well it does me good to hear you're becoming an independent young man. Here's a few quid for the tram, I don't want you getting home too late." He placed some money squarely in my hand before walking toward the exit, he turned around at the last second to say, "Be home by supper, for your mum's sake." I gave him a smile and a nod, he did so back and disappeared into the crowd.

It was good to see the displays refurbished and added onto in recent years. I remember at age five, during a school trip, many of the collections were in disrepair or shoddily kept.

There were some new exhibits from Korea and Malaya, but what really caught my interest was the incoming collection from Rhodesia; a satiating hold-over until the new wing of the museum was completed, supposedly with a cinema, and a display for experimental robotics technologies. Very exciting.

I was humbled by these collections, of being surrounded by the planes, tanks, ships, guns, and uniforms which men from my own city once took the reigns of, to conquer and protect for the empire; it sometimes leaves me wanting to help pull the chain, do my part, enlist in the Royal Air Force like father did, but mother discourages it, says there are no more wars for Britain to fight, father, depending on his mood, may sometimes agree with her, says "*unless our home faces direct invasion, it may not be wise for the empire to engage in war for a time*". They told me I was simply too young to understand.

"Excuse me young man, this exhibit is closed." Called a twenty-something red-haired member of the museum staff.
"The Rhodesia exhibit is closed to the public, you can't be here." He said in an Irish cadence.

"Why, is something broken?" I asked.

"No, nothing is broken, but all trade with Rhodesia has been halted. This exhibit is to be shut down until further notice from the higher ups. We don't want to be encouraging sympathy for them, you know." Said the man escorting me out into the hall.

"But why? Isn't Rhodesia one of our colonies?" I pointed out.

"Young man, Rhodesia is a gangrenous appendage that refuses to come off cleanly. It's not something a boy like you should be learning about by this point."

"But why? My father's told me all about them, says there aren't any finer soldiers in all the commonwealth than the Rhodesians."

"That so? Does your father actually agree with what Rhodesia's doing? Haven't you heard the news?"
"My father says the news is nothing but propaganda."

"You listen to everything your father tells you, boy? I'd watch what you say. It's talk like that what gets you in trouble."

I found that the man had actually escorted me out of the museum entirely, and upon ending his sentence, had shut the door closed.

I pressed back to attempt reentry, but there he was, guarding the door, holding it firm so I couldn't make my way back in, mocking me from behind the glass window.

"What's the big idea!?" I yelled as I tried to push the door open.

"Move along, chav. I'd say you've overstayed your welcome. Come back when your head is clear of that garbage." He laughed.

I rammed the door with my elbow, forcing my way in, running through the place while he shouted and chased after me. I bolted behind a tank, and took cover behind a row of uniforms. My attempts at hiding were no good, I was pulled by my collar, and dragged out to a security office. Apparently I had damaged the door attempting to force my way in, or so I overheard, I could also hear him repeatedly say to his boss "*little racist*" and "*stealing*" as if trying to conjure up a story to justify what became a lifetime banning from the museum.

"You best not show your face around here, chav!" He yelled as I was forced along the exit path by a guard. I pulled a stone from the garden and threw it at him with full force, actually shattering the glass window of the door and giving him a fright, 'think he may've even cut his hand.

"Fuck off back to Ireland, you damned pikey!" I yelled at him before running free of the guard who'd given up his chase moments in.

My senses were tense, there was a heat of embarrassment and anger burning behind my eyes. I thought of brutalizing that usher for what felt like a humiliation of me. All this trouble for something so petty and stupid.

"The nerve of that-! Telling me I've overstayed my welcome! I swear I should walk back and-" I slammed my hands against a street sign and shook it furiously, I started kicking it, accidentally striking a parked car, setting off its alarm.
"No, I'm not taking this standing-!" I turned around, ripped a hefty branch off of a tree, and began walking back up to the museum. I eyed the floor for the man who forced me out, spying him facing away. Ideal. I approached, tapping him on the shoulder.
He turned to face me with a scowl, but before he could speak, I swiped him across the face with the branch. Not one of my finest moments, perhaps, but right it did feel.

To the precinct I was sent, too young to face serious charges, especially as a first time offender. The way I saw it, they give you one free crime to commit as a kid, might as well use it for something that matters before you're too old. That's just how I saw it, never thought I would, but now that I have, I understand the satisfaction.

Father had to pick me up, fill out some documents, and enroll me in an anger counseling program for two months, but we got to drive home that night.
It was silent, all but the rain and the radio tuned so quietly it hardly broke the silence.

"Garrath-" Father said, breaking the tension. "-What got into you, son. I left you alone at a museum of all things, picking you up from the police station was the least of my expectations."

"I'm sorry, dad. I didn't mean for this to trouble you, but a man insulted me, you taught me never to let myself be pushed around if I could help it, 'taught me not to tolerate an injustice, this man, he tried to force me from the museum for no good reason!"

"No *good* reason, but there was a reason?" Father asked.

"Oh he was speaking nonsense, one of those politically sensitive types, but I told him what you told me, and he kicked me out for it! Insulted me, and dragged me by my collar!" Father sighed solemnly.

"Son-" He hesitated. "There are some things you just can't say in public that we say at home. Our country isn't what it used to be. People are a lot more-" He restrained himself from swearing. "-sensitive nowadays. The era of Churchill died with him, there's new people in charge now, they decide what is rule. It just so happens that our opinions are-" He searched for the right word. "-unpleasant to them. Some ideas best go unsaid, son. It's time to leave the empire behind and just try to focus on the UK for now."

"But dad, the empire-"

"What empire, Garrath? The empire has been dying since World War Two. Another colony just broke away four days ago, it seems a new one breaks away every week! Soon there'll be nothing left. Centuries of conquest and achievement undone in the span of years! If only it ended there-" He slowed the car onto the side of the street, double parking it.

On the street was a shop that appeared to be an asian lounge of some sort, two Pakistani men stepped out and got into a luxurious car parked a few vehicles ahead of ours.

"Back in my day-" Father started. "-we reaped the wealth and bounty of lands like India, Persia, and Africa. We brought them technology and industry they'd never seen. Now in our weakened state, they reap the riches and lifeblood of our dying corpse. What a time it was, indeed. But it's not your time, Garrath. You need to understand that. You need to let the past die. Hope toward the future, ensure you even have a future to hope for."

Texas, Kirk Ranch
November 9 1966
|Del Kirk|

We'd gotten a knock at the door early morning, 'round 6 a.m.

Pops and I were in the middle of breakfast, ma was at the dishes. We'd planned to reap the big crop for the Harvest Festival, but things took a different turn that day. Pop answered the door.

"Howdy bud. How may I help ya?" Pops asked.

"Mr.Kirk, am I correct?" Asked the well-dressed, official looking man.

"Darn right. Del Kirk Senior-" I ran up beside him. "-this is my son, Junior. Now what brings you to our porch this morning?"

"Well, Mr.Kirk-" He shuffled some papers on his clipboard. "-I'm here on behalf of the federal government because it appears you have what we'd consider a surplus quantity of firearms."

"Surplus? Well, I certainly wouldn't call it a surplus, but I do have a gun for about every necessity, plus a spare: Long rifle, carbine, shotgun, and revolver, two of each."

"Yes, indeed. See, under new law, we consider any value greater than one firearm per legal adult a surplus, and in event of a surplus we'd like to encourage a trade-in for compensation." Pops was taken aback, but was quick to dismiss the stranger.

"Well I appreciate your encouragement, but I'm quite happy with my surplus, sir. Thanks for stopping by-" Pops tried to shut the door, but the man caught it with his foot.

"Well, I'm afraid it's not that simple, sir. The *administration of common-sense firearm safety* has put a ban on surplus firearms for civilian households, and it'd be in your best interest to turn them in for full compensation."

"What if I refuse?"

"I'm afraid they'll be seized, and you could face both a fine and jail time." Pops was in shock. "Now, understand, sir, it's not without cause. Understand, especially in this state, with the assassination of our former President, we're just trying to take preventative measures for our current Presidents safety, and the safety of every citizen."

"Well there must be some kind of work around." Pops offered.

"Unless you're a licensed firearms retailer authorized by the federal government, or the US military, I'm afraid there is no exception to the Firearm Surplus Act." Pops stared the stranger down and patted me on the shoulder.

"Junior, go finish your breakfast. Pop needs to have a word with this man here." I understood and ran back to the breakfast table before he shut the door, stepping outside.

Pops used to watch the presidents talks on tv, 'said he was no good, and he was worried things were going to change.

We were in Dallas the day the President was shot; I was five, but I remember it like it was yesterday. I heard a loud crack, ma covered me, and pops tried to lead us away from the street, I didn't know what was happening, but I knew something had happened. Ma says the new President might've done it so he could become president, pops says considering how much he's changing the country, it wouldn't surprise him.

"Get off my property! Get, you son'va bitch!" I could hear pops shout from behind the solid oak door. "Unbelievable!" Pops shouted, slamming the door behind him. "There's no chance we're the only ones who won't stand for this! Shannon!" Pops walked over to Ma and me, he looked at her. "They're saying we've got to give up our guns by the end of the month, Shannon. We either do or they'll send the feds to come take them, along with our house and our son!" Ma shook when she heard that last line, asking him why. "If we refuse they'll sign us down as dangerous. *Unfit to raise a child*!"

"Pops, I don't want them to take me away from you." I said clutching my father's shirt.

"I won't let them, boy. No one's taking anything from us. Shannon, we've got to talk. Junior, finish your breakfast."

Ma and pop went upstairs so I wouldn't be caught up in the conversation, they didn't want to scare me, but I could still hear them through the creaky wood ceiling.

"Shannon, we can't take this standing down, this has got to violate the constitution." Pop said.

"They're just putting a limit on how many we can own, it might not count-" Ma offered.

"*The right of the people to keep and bear arms shall-not-be-infringed*! As in they cannot encroach upon our legal right to possess arms capable of combating the government should it ever turn against us! And you know what? I'd say we're damn near close to that!"

"Del, we'd still get to keep some 'our guns, this isn't worth losing the life we've made, or our son!"

"This isn't where it'll stop! It's a never ending slope easing us into total submission! This is the land of the free, and in the last few years we've seen over half the money in all our pockets go to the governments commie experiment; what if I don't want to pay for some illegal's house? You heard they're aborting unborn children, Shannon? It's disgustin', and our money's funding it! It's a damn slippery slope toward satanic socialism! We've seen the fed grow bigger and stronger while we become more and more dependent on 'em! We've seen our youth sucked into meat grinders of war; do you want to raise our boy just so he can die in Korea or Vietnam? I fought the World War so my boy wouldn't have to, but if he's got to defend his home, damn right I want him to have the firepower necessary to do so! Believe me when I say they'll come for the boy eventually, and by that point we'll be totally powerless to stop it, the best-, the only time to act is right damn now!" Pops took a long breath. "I'm sorry, Shannon. I want nothing but the best for you and Junior, and this feels like a damn mountain to climb." I heard him drag a chair across the floor and a creak as he took a seat. "I'm gonna stop this, Shannon, you hear. We're not taking this without a fight, and I'm damn sure few others will either. I'm gonna go around town telling all our neighbors what the hell is happening, and then I'm taking this to town hall. We're gonna keep living free even if I need to fight to earn it back, I've done it before, and our founding fathers did it before me. Tyranny will not reign over this land, no tyrant will ever tell me how to live my life."

Pops and ma came down the stairs. Ma came first, giving me a kiss on my forehead.

Pops came down the stairs polishing a revolver, and emptying the cylinder. He walked over to me, placing the revolver in my hand; it was mighty heavy. He said to me,

"Son, times are changing, and you need to be prepared for whatever the future might bring. No matter what happens, no matter who tries to tell you what you can and can't do, never forget that tyrants, be they giants, or just like you and me, tyrants are still made of flesh and bone." He placed a bullet in the palm of my hand.
"Ma and I are going to teach you how to protect your home, and you're gonna practice every day until no man or beast is beyond your capability. Is that right, boy?" I nodded in agreement. "Good. Shannon, give him his first lesson, I need to ring the neighbors, there's not a moment to waste."
Pops knelt to my level, I kept the bullet in one hand while he helped me to hold up the revolver with my other; his hands were clasped over mine as he prayed.
"Dear Lord, let this boy grow to be fast and accurate. Let his aim be true, and his hands faster than those who would wish to destroy him. Grant to him the strength and vision to protect his home and that which he holds most dearly. So shall it be done."

Massachusetts, Rockport Town
December 10 1966
|Percy Holiday|

"Mom? Mom, when're we gonna have dinner?" I said tugging on my mother's dress. She was smoking with one hand, and holding the phone with the other, talking to a friend of hers and trying to shoo me away with her leg. "Mom, I'm hungry." I groaned.

"Hold on just a moment, sweetheart. Don't go anywhere." She said smoothly into the phone with a giggle before coming down to my level, and hissing at me in a hushed tone. "Mommy's busy, we'll have dinner later!" Her irish accent breaking through.

"But mom, I'm hungry now."

"Spoiled little-" She mumbled, digging through her purse. "See this? It's like money, go to the store and buy yourself something." She said shoving me a food stamp before picking her phone back up, twirling the cord with her cigarette grasping fingers. "-Sorry about that, love."

"*Good grief.*" I thought as I pulled my rain boots on and zipped up a light jacket. I stepped out to find it showering. I pulled my hood up, and started trending toward the corner store two blocks down. The neighborhood could be a little scary at night, there's nothing between my block and the few shoreside stores but dilapidated, boarded up apartment buildings, even though during the day, I really liked it, especially a day like this with the dark, murky, greyish-blue sky, and the smell of sea mist in the air blended into each rain drop. I bet most kids would be upset to have to walk in this weather, but I'm getting familiar with it; 'startin' to like it better out here in fact, the air's fresher, no one bothers me-

"'Ey *Holly-day*!"

At least not most of the time.

I turned around to be met with the two Gambino boys and another of their friends; they were middle school kids, at least four years older than me.

"Where you goin' in this weatha', Holly-day? Goin' to the store? What's you got on you?" They started for my pockets, pulling out the food stamp. "Aw, no cash?" They laughed.

"His mom's broke." Said one of the brothers.

"Oh, but she's hot. Think she'd suck my dick for a dollar?"

I shouldn't of let 'em get to me, Mom and I didn't even get along, but she's still my mom, an insult to her was an insult to me; I didn't care if she felt it, I hated that I felt it. I punched that boy below the belt, and tried to run for it, but they chased after me. I slipped in the rain, and they held me down.

"You're gonna wish you didn't do that, *Holly-day*." Giovanni, the boy I punched, pulled out a pocket knife. "I'm gonna give you a reminder who's top dog 'round these parts, you little mick bastard!" He cut my jacket and lifted up my shirt, the cold of the rain masked the feel of the blade as he pressed it against my stomach. I clenched my eyes in some hope it'd save me somehow.

"Hey! What're you doin' ta that kid!" I could hear stomping through the puddles. "You get offa' him, you sons a' bitches!" The rain was blurring my vision, but I could see two other boys knock over the Gambinos while their friend bolted off.
"You get the hell outta' here! Ya hear me! We catch you bustin' up kids again, and you're a fockin' corpse!" One of the boys yelled as I heard the Gambino's boots splashing away in the water. "Christ. You alright, kid?" One of the boys asked, offering me a hand up.

"Why'd you save me?" I asked in actual astonishment someone did. He kinda chuckled.

"Well what was we supposed to do, let 'em carve you like a pumpkin? We were just heading back from the store, and caught what was goin' down. I'm Holden, my parents named me like the book character. This here's my buddy, Tyler."

"'Ey, little man. We know them Gambinos from school, always causing trouble. Always." Said Tyler.

"I'm Percy. I was just going to the store-" As I fixed myself up, I noticed my food stamp dissolving on the ground as the rain beat down on it.

"Lost your cash, huh? We know how it is, our folks ain't exactly loaded either. Here-" Holden said offering me a few bills. "Go on, take it, come on, we'll go with ya." They escorted me to the store where I tried to dry myself off. I looked around the shelves for something I could buy to fill me up, Tyler heard my stomach rumbling.

"Yeah, you know it. I need to get me some dinner. Holden, any chance we can get something for us to eat too?" Tyler asked.

"You just ate, you dumb bastard, this kid got jumped, come on." Tyler raised his hands in compliance. "Hey kid, sorry uh- *Percy*, what're you in the mood for?"

"I don't know, I'll take anything." I said.

"Heh, well a soda is anything, a candy bar is anything, what do you like to eat, little man? Don't be shy." I looked up at the deli menu; I was in the mood for something warm.

"Um, can I get a hot turkey sandwich?"

"Turkey sandwich?" Tyler asked, sounding half interested, and half hungry.

"Is that not good?" I said unsure of myself. Holden just laughed.

"No, there's nothing wrong with it, kid. Hey Mr.Randazzo, we'll take a turkey sandwich, and a soda." The Deliman said "*sure thing*", and got to prepping the order. Holden took a soda cup, and walked over to the fountain with me. "I'm guessing your 'rents don't bother enough to make sure you get to the store okay, huh?"

"Mom was just busy, she told me to buy myself dinner from the store." Holden nodded his head disapprovingly.

“Just your mom, huh?”

“Yeah, just her. Dad left a long time ago, before I can even remember.” I answered. Holden gritted his teeth, and looked at Tyler who also seemed to be nodding disapprovingly.

“Hey Percy, do you want to hang out tomorrow? Maybe we can get lunch or something, our treat. We’ll share it.”

“Oh, yeah! That sounds great!” I said eagerly, happy to be treated so generously.

“We’ll ring the bell, or if you want, we can just wait outside for you.”

“*Order up.*” Called the Deliman.

“You can ring the bell, just let me know around what time.” I said.

“How’s about noon? Sound good, buddy?” Holden asked.

“That sounds good. Thanks again, guys, for everything.”

“Don’t mention it, bud. We’ve got to look out for each other. Come on, we’ll walk you home.”

Chapter 2
California, Berkeley
June 27 1967
|Augustus Doctor|

"Let us make one fact unmistakably clear; every single one of you in this room is far too weak!"
The Commander addressed the audience of students. "I know you're all probably thinking 'oh yeah, every single one but me', no! Not a single one of you is sufficiently strong enough in character, physicality, or in mental power to, at this moment, fix the problems

we face today as Americans. You lack discipline, liberal society by its very nature opposes discipline and regimentation. You lack strength, your fathers, if they in fact worked hard, laborious jobs, have placed you here so that you need not toil to exhaustion as they do, falsely believing that an easier life is equivalent to a better life. And it is here where the greatest swindling takes place, feeding information into you that amounts to the opinions and warped worldviews of some liberal professor. I ask you to merely contrast your lives, the lives of pampered white-students with the privilege of either wealth or intelligence to justify your place in this room, contrast that with the life of a negro in the ghetto; they are poorer, they are uneducated, they live in regular danger of each other. They do not have the luxuries you do, but this in turn has given them something even greater than wealth and knowledge, that advantage is hardship; hardship is the fire in which character and strength are forged. Your parents perhaps knew hardship, mine was a generation shaped by the great depression, I and my contemporaries knew nothing but hardship, and it made us strong men capable of fighting a war. Knowledge and wealth are tremendous assets, assets which have contributed to making the white race perhaps the most successful race on the planet, but always, until fairly recently, has this knowledge and wealth needed to come at great cost for all who possess it, but not you. To you, it was merely handed, because your fathers endured a hardship so great that they wished you would never need to see it. When wealth and knowledge are acquired without hardship, it breeds arrogance, decadence, and weakness. I look around this room, and that is what I see; I'm not proud to say it, I feel no satisfaction from it, it makes me feel downright miserable to know just how much society has neutered you, even outside of your homes in these colleges and cushy jobs, this is not the life men were meant to live!"

The Commander took a pause to shuffle through his papers which he handed to me at his side. “Pass these out, please.” He said to me before returning to his speech. "In my party we destroy weakness, we promote strength, we reject the degeneracy of the modern world, and embrace traditional adherence to virtue; we are men, we are white men, we are white American men! The sons of pioneers, explorers, hunters, and warriors who conquered and created this beautiful country we now possess, and which we are at risk of letting slip from our hands as we grow lazy, indulgent, and weak! Even the Communists know this in their own countries, they see us as the fat, overfed capitalists with no restraint on our desire for excess, we weren't always like this! Capitalism too has run rampant and devolved into a disgusting consumerist philosophy of possession and indulgence, slaving away for flashy goods, instead of working hard for that which actually matters. We encourage each one of you, those of you at military age especially, to join our party in a protective vanguard for White America, the details of which are in these pamphlets being handed out by my up-and-coming right-hand-man, Mr.Doctor; He is a Vietnam veteran, having served three tours to keep his country safe, and has chosen to continue that job back home where it is needed most. He's a strong young man who's seen intensive combat, and keeps himself sharp for the day the war comes to America, and that day will come, gentlemen! If our party meets you as too extreme, if you're too afraid of being even remotely associated with the word *'Nat-zee'*, then for your own sake, the sake of your children and your country, prepare yourself! Harden yourself! Be someone worth following, someone worth looking up to, for the sake of those you care about. In you rests the fate of our future. Thank you all very much."

The audience rose in a blend of applause and boo's, the good Commander stepped away from the podium. I finished handing out the pamphlets before stepping backstage to meet with him.

My job upon joining his party consisted of low-tier public relations, he quickly promoted me to a captain and editor of our party magazine, the position had opened up because the former editor had been outed as a Communist trying to infiltrate the party.
I've been the printed voice of the party for the last few months, and the Commander, as always, remained the guiding spoken voice. We

saw eye to eye much more than I'd initially anticipated, him teaching me of things I sensed but could never articulate.

He held sympathy for my history in 'Nam, having served in the Second World War himself, he knew what it was like to get sucked up into wanting to do everything in your power to fight the enemies of your country, only to realize they weren't truly *our* enemies. Damn right we hate the communists, but why does Vietnam affect us? Why did Germany affect us? We ought strike those who strike us, and it's felt in recent years that our aim has been far off.

"Another day, another protest, huh, kid?" The Commander asked as he lit his pipe, addressing to me the riotous party of liberals and communists waiting to harass us outside.

"There were some jeers from the crowd, but by the end of it most were cheering."

"They call ***me*** prejudice, yet those who shout slurs against me tend to be the ones prejudging before they've heard what I've had to say. Seems those leftists truly believe me to be nothing more than a soulless monster, some sort of ***villain.***"

"Well, sir, our optics are rather-" I chose my words carefully. "-extreme. With a party bearing the name '***Nazi***', we ought have expected no less a reaction."

"And yet you've joined our ranks, Doctor."

"I believed in what you said, sir. I had no idea who you were or what party you represented, only that you seemed to understand the problems I felt better than any politician could. It made no difference to me if you touted yourself a Nazi or a Socialist, your message made sense."

"And what is my message if not the message of American National Socialism? '***Nazi***' doesn't seem to mean anything anymore besides being a slur for racially-conscious whites; we seem to be the only racial group who is berated for the slightest mention of not even pride, but recognition of our race. The core of my ideology is not hate, I hardly give a damn of other races, be they good or bad, all I desire is to protect my own, and only do I hate those who wish harm upon my kind. Of course I still hate, but without a deadly hate for that which threatens what you love, love is without value, it becomes nothing but an empty catchphrase for queers and cowards. We seek the protection, and betterment of our White-American race through application of science and ancestral moral doctrine. We are one people whose combined lives make-up a healthy and functional national body; that is National Socialism." He responded. I smiled.

"And that's the objective that has kept me by your side, sir."

"If only others could look past the slander as you do, son."

"Perhaps if we adopted a more attractive title, sir. As you said, '***Nazi***' has acquired a new meaning in the minds of the majority; most will shut us out entirely before they've heard a word we had to say."

"I didn't adopt our party name without reason, son. In part I thought it would be a brilliant move to garner attention, the shock-factor of a Nazi party in the US, but more than anything else, I never believed in holding back the truth, of sugar-coating a message, and it wouldn't matter if you did regardless, because your opposition will still hurl upon you every accusation imaginable, until in the public-eye you ***are*** a Nazi, just one without an honest and effective message. By the end if I could change the minds of but one percent in a crowd of one thousand, that's still ten men. Ten men is good, though I do wish we could reach more."

"We're going to need more stormtroopers, sir. If and when war comes, we're not going to fare well with only 500 men as a faction." I said to him.

"I wouldn't be so sure, there's power in that concentration of organization. How many other parties do you believe will be organizing with the same strength we are?"

"I really couldn't say, sir, that's what concerns me. I'd rather we overestimate our opponents than underestimate them. We should really begin militarizing." He nodded and took his pipe from his mouth, pointing with it.

"We are not yet a military organization. If we start stockpiling weapons, you can very well believe the feds will come on down and take them by force. We'll stand our ground, and they'll wipe us out right then and there. We're not prepared yet, one day, but not today."

"Yes sir." I thought for a minute. "What if we encouraged personal militarization, as you said, *prepare yourselves*. 1000 personally armed men are better than just 500. Think of it as our militia. I can personally organize training exercises, and enforce discipline to the party." He smiled at me.

"Your initiative alone isn't what's gotten you as far as you have, Augustus, it's your will to power. You take a thought, put it into action, and get it done even if it's difficult, grueling even. You get the job done. Keep it up." He took a smoke. "I'll put forward the memo: The party encourages all members to arm up."

Arlington Virginia, Party Headquarters
July 26 1967
|Augustus Doctor|

"-What do we do when the mag is empty!?"

"Fix a bayonet, sir!" My unit shouted back at me. A company of 100 fit, battle ready new recruits taking the rifles we encouraged them to buy, and affixing their bayonets with perfect synchronicity.

"Now charge!" Row by row, ten charged toward the tire dummies we'd set up. I'd stopped one, a long-haired recruit. "What's this, son?" I said pulling at his braid.

"I-I'm sorry, sir."

"You know what this is in war, son? A damn fuse!" I slipped out a lighter, and threatened to ignite his hair. "Is that how you want to go?"

"No sir!"

"Get out of here, don't come back until you have a proper haircut, Fuse."

"Yes sir!" He said with a salute before running for the road.

"The rest of you, next row, charge!"

"Mister Doctor-" A voice called out from behind me. "Commander needs to have a word with you." I nodded.

"Until I return, I want laps around the headquarters, no breaks until I return!" I shouted to my company.

"Yes sir!" They shouted back in unison.

I stepped in through the front door, and walked up to the commander's office, knocking before peering in.

"Commander, you called for me?"

“I believe there are spies in our ranks.” He said abruptly as he rifled through the filing cabinets behind him.

“Spies, sir? Who?”

“I can’t say for sure, but recent intel indicates to me that the Feds may very well be attempting to plant seeds of dissent in the party, and compromise our operations.”

“But why?”

“The *why* is simple enough; The US government goes through periods of change, and this most recent shift under that liberal commie is driving the nation in the opposite direction of our party. We had our chance to decide this country’s path in the fifties, but we’ve steered too far off course to correct.” The Commander sorted through a number of files, shredding some.

“What are you shredding, sir?”

“Documents with information only you and I share, information which I will not let fall into the hands of our enemies. You know what I am referring to?”

“Yes sir.” He must’ve been referring to our weapon caches, our gold reserves, and our bunkers for post-collapse operations.

“If I were to make a bet-” The Commander said. “-I’d square the assumption on one of our older members, Hurley, Peterson, or Nemo, I especially have a strong feeling that fellow is a jew.”

“P-Perhaps, sir, but-” I responded, but the commander immediately cut me off.

“-Now our party is laid smack in the middle of a regime that very much does not want us to exist, and will do away with us in a manner that'll make it look as if we've simply lost influence or disbanded." He paused for a moment to ensure the door was locked. "I need you to cease recruitment and militia activities until we've weeded out the traitors. Our numbers are solid and our cohesion is unbreakable, but we cannot afford a breach."

"Yes sir, I'll give the order."

I returned to my unit, allowed them to rest, and dismissed them from training. We sent a letter out to our militia members informing them to continue their regimentation and training at home while we prepared better training equipment, a guise to cover up our investigation of the vipers in our ranks.

As the weeks passed, the Commander and I narrowed the culprits to twenty men, all or any number of which could have been an agent operating against us.
I'd begin meeting one on one with individual recruits to both train and observe them for suspicious activities, it took time, and by the end of the month I hadn't found anyone who particularly stood out from our usual demographic among the fifteen I managed to meet with. It did worry me, left me wondering how safe we were in an increasingly unwelcoming country.

Virginia, Arlington
August 25 1967
|Augustus Doctor|

We knew we were hated, we knew there were people out there who would do us great harm if they had the chance, but no one thought it would ever actually happen.

A legal suit, a minor fight, or a clash in the streets, we had our brushes with trouble, but otherwise we were immortals, at least we felt like we were, but I never let my guard down. I tried to do the same for the Commander; I was there to keep him outside the range of a bullet, or take one for him if need be.

"Alright, Doctor, I don't think I'll be needing security for this wing of my day." The Commander told me on a cool summer night.

"Are you certain, sir? It's no trouble to me, the party's my life, this is all I have to do."

"I'm sure, son. This is my neighborhood, no one would dare stir trouble with me here. I'll just be dropping off some laundry before heading home. I expect to see you first thing tomorrow, son."

There was a subtle buzz in the air from the laundromat's neon sign, it and the moon just barely illuminating the scene which I scrutinized for any unsavory characters. It was peaceful, one of those nights where the only life you could hear were the crickets.

"Yes sir."

With that, I was dismissed. He stepped into the laundromat, and I located my car parked not too far away. I climbed in and tried the ignition; the engine was stalling a bit, which was strange to me because I'd just bought it, so I popped the hood, deciding to see what the issue was. To my disturbance, I found the wires and hoses of my car mangled, leaking, as if someone had tried to sabotage my vehicle. I grew concerned, more so as I heard the clicking of the Commanders steps as he exited the laundromat. I turned to see him searching for his keys when suddenly a deafening crack broke the night air. He staggered and clutched his chest with one hand, blood oozing through his white shirt.

"Commander!" I ran to him. He turned to see me, and pointed up to the distance, the source of the bullet. He fell to the ground, I clutched onto him. "Stay with me, sir! Please!" He continued to point to the source, blood spurted from his mouth. I looked to the distance to see a man on a roof sling a rifle over his shoulder, and retreat into the dark.

The Commander grasped my shirt collar, he was choking on his own blood. He coughed heavily. Before he grew cold, I heard him utter in a guttural gasp two last words,
"-Mister Doctor."

England, Birmingham
April 20 1968
|Garrath King|

Father hasn't been doing very well, mother's even worse it'd seem. Father's work at the lock-smithery had been replacing employees with cheaper imports; he'd been forced to take a paycut to keep his job. The bank has been hounding us, repossessed fathers car as collateral, now he takes the tram.

Less food at home, I try to eat as little as possible to leave mother what she needs, she'd gotten sick recently, and with our budget we hardly have the funds to treat her.

I'd lost my work as a shop clerk when the boss discovered my mate, Thomas, had been stealing from the till to feed his heroin addiction, 'pinned it on us both, left my pockets empty.

I took the public transport to the city where I'd spy the immigrant boys, their parents supposedly came here to escape poverty, yet every one that I'd see would flash off his wealth with pristine designer-shirts, and shiny new cars.
They'd occupy entire neighborhoods, turning them into extravagant versions of their homes overseas, while my family, who's history has known only England, withers in the shade of the weed which has sprouted upon our land, sucking away our lifesblood, and pushing drugs onto us. Not a childhood friend I know hasn't succumbed to the black tar poison introduced to our neighborhood.

England no longer feels like the home of the English, it is a treasure trove to be plundered by those who see the opportunity to exploit. I fear we are now the unwanted.

I picked a fight with Thomas's dealer, a Persian or Palestinian I believe; 'was attempting to cut him off from his source, but to my shock this nearly got me arrested for a potential hate crime. New laws have left some afraid to protect themselves, afraid to fight back, lest big-brother government step in, and finish you off itself.

I walked a thin line, I did. My family was desperate, and I couldn't sit idle while my people, my country, was set upon and looted. I saw an opportunity to take back what had been taken from us.
I started off small at first, snatching a wallet, using it to buy medicine for my mother, but as I continued, I wondered why I shouldn't do the same for all those English families out there. Mine were just one of several in a long line of similar troubles.

I was an avid climber and lockpick. Thanks to my fathers trade as a locksmith I learned how the most secure and complex locks functioned, whilst I taught myself to scale brick and stone with little more than a centimeter of ledge, it became necessary to dodge the coppers time and again; my taste for trouble never quite vanished.

I had the skill, I had the desire, all that remained was the will to take action, and truthfully, I was afraid, but if I abstained from action now, then nothing would change, I'd be nothing more than a spectator to the death of my home, helpless.
Yes, perhaps I may fail, perhaps I'll get caught, but I will not surrender before I've even begun! As with serving overseas, you must risk life and limb, but all is done in the name of duty to king and country. I would fear not death, I would fear not brutality, and I certainly would fear not petty incarceration. For my people, I must act.

I'd take from the wealthy, give to the needy; like Robin Hood, I saw myself; I was a people's soldier. Others began calling me *Young John Bull*, protecting the English, and pushing back against the migrant invaders on our soil, but one day things got too uncomfortably close.

I'd believed the apartment to be empty, that the occupants had left for work, that I'd have all the time necessary to sweep the place, and vacate before anyone would return.

I picked my way through the door, making as though my key were stuck to mask my task. I gathered the typical valuables: Jewelry, loose cash, expensive clothing, but every now and then I'd find myself met with a safe, this was one of those instances.
It was a simple locking bolt mechanism that father had worked on prior, there was a way to pick the lock without need for a combination, but it would take time and precision, both of which I had, or so I thought.

I had secured two of the three lock pins when the sound of a squeaking door sent a cold jolt down my spine. Someone had entered the house.

The rooms were clearly disheveled, they'd know somebody had been here.

"Hello? Anyone here?" I heard a boy about my age call out in a typical anglo-pakistani accent. I heard the unmistakable sound of a piece of metal clang up against wood, a pipe or perhaps a baton. I'd need to hide my face and navigate my way out.

I wrapped a scarf around my head, and tracked their movement about the apartment. As I heard him move into one room, I'd move too, putting more distance between us before I'd reached the door, only to be grabbed by another, this one a man perhaps twice my age.

I headedbutted the man before dashing to the nearest room I could, locking the door behind me, both attempting to knock it down. I was trapped. The only exit was a window, I'd need to scale my way down, I didn't have many options.

Swiping the window open, I grasped on tightly to the slightest ledge, lowering myself into an alley. A loud wooden crack indicated to me that the door had been broken down, but I'd almost reached the ground. I leaped off to see one of the men peering out the window before pulling himself back in. I ran down the alley and soon heard the whirring of a motorbike behind me. I was being pursued, I could hear someone yell,

"Get him! It's Johnny Bull!"

If they caught me, that'd be the end of the line.

"***Run***" was all my mind would tell me.

I was met with a wall, one I knew I could climb, but feared I would not have enough time to.

It didn't matter, it was my only means of escape.

I climbed higher and higher, hearing the motorbike reach the wall, and stop, by then I was far beyond their reach, a good ten metres high. Climbing over the edge and onto the roof, I finally felt relief, but before I'd been able to appreciate this moments solace, the ground or rather glass beneath me began to crack, dropping me into a dark, seldom used storage room.

My body ached from the drop. I picked glass from my hands and legs, unwrapping my face, and leaving behind my loot in the event of a search. I even held with me the bloodied glass shards to dispose of them.

I felt sick, shaking from uneased nerves and injuries, so much so that I hadn't realized someone had been speaking loudly in the other room.

"-*It is almost comparable to a curse, that the very nature of politics is that of a fixation on events current, with little foresight on the evils to come from so reckless a decision.*"
The voice spoke in a stern, instructive tone. I sought to find the source of the speech, leaving the dark room for the brightly illuminated hall where the muffled yet booming voice continued.
"-*I was recently approached by a citizen of my own town, he was not a spoiled elitist or the vision of some fascist, on the contrary, he like many of us served in the second world war to defeat fascism. This was an average middle aged man who worked a very modest occupation. He said to me, 'If only the means were available to me, I would turn my back to this land and never look back. I have a wife and son whom I cherish dearly, but for whom I can see no happy future in England. Mark my words, in two decades time, this land will no longer belong to the sons of England.'*"

The voice grew louder as I came closer to the source.

"*I'm sure you've all prepared your personal outrage. What heinous bigotry. What heinous manner to repeat such a discussion in a room of governance. To that, I say we simply do not have the right to ignore such a statement. For the image of the average Englishman to approach me, his member of parliament, with the fear that England will no longer be a secure home for the future of his family, to shrug it off as if negligible. We do not have the right. Across England we are seeing a dramatic change unlike any ever before seen in our entire history as a nation. Not since the Norman conquests have demographics across entire areas of our land shifted so drastically. Never before have projections shown such significant immigrant and immigrant descendant population growth set to exponentially rise over the next half century, and already to overtake London. It is with great urgency that we must act in regards to this future, and avert our eyes from the distractions of the present, knowing full well that we are only delaying our present difficulties for our children and their children to face tenfold, if even our children get the chance to resolve them. By importing incompatible foreign populations in such great quantity, we are in essence entrusting the fate of our home to the actions of men of whom we know nothing. That which we temporarily mend today will have no assurance of being mended in the long term."*

I found the door to the speaker's room, and peered in, it was packed with well dressed political types, the man speaking was a gentleman politician in his mid to late fifties.

"So often before death, we see men fall into madness. I suppose that is precisely what we believe ourselves to be, a dying empire gone mad. How absolutely mad, for us to so quickly accept death when time and time again we've beaten it back with our own strength, own means, and own determination! Instead we now seek a population to relieve us of our tired duty, to replace us as the occupants of this land we've seemingly grown so encumbered by that we'd wish not even burden our children with it, this duty our great grandfathers passed down to us, and their fathers did to them! It is deeply concerning that a stigma has seemingly arisen amongst our people, a fear of reprisal for simply speaking publicly the very words I've expressed with you today. Already we see our fellow men and women become the persecuted in the drastically changed communities of which they've suddenly become the unwanted minorities of. Yet there remains a fear to question the direction our nation has taken, as if the captain is steering blindly yet punishes the man who questions his course. For better or for worse, we are on the verge of a dramatic change. Given the current climate of our state, I am filled with foreboding; Like the Austrian, I seem to see the Gates of Vienna under siege, coming upon us here through our own volition. To do nothing now would be disastrous, to hold our tongues of this truth would be the ultimate betrayal."

As the speaker concluded his speech, the room applauded him, he gave a bow, and excused himself from the room. I ran from the door, and took shelter in a closet as to not be noticed.
The speaker stepped out, shutting the door behind him, stopping to stare at his hand, then at the doorknob: Blood. He glanced at the ground, and traced a trail of blood drops on the beige carpet to the closet door. He approached the door, placing his hand on the doorknob.

"May I ask who's in there?" The speaker said. I simply responded by nudging open the door to reveal myself. "My lord, boy! Are you alright? What are you doing here? What's happened to you?" Before I answered, he gestured me out, inspecting my wounds. "Come, come, you can wash yourself off in the lavatory. I'll fetch you some bandages."

He led me to the restroom where I disposed of the glass, and washed my hands; the sink ran murky red from the blood. He returned with wrapping gauze, and asked me to hold out my hands so he could bandage them.

"I have many questions for you, I certainly hope you have the courtesy to answer them truthfully."

"I enjoyed your speech, sir." I said abruptly. He looked up.

"Well thank you, boy. How about we begin with your name, then." I was hesitant to give away my name.

"Johnny, sir. My name's Johnny."

"Well, Johnny, let's proceed from there. I see you stuck around for my speech, but what brought you here to begin with? I don't assume broken glass is typical of a front door entrance."

"I fell through a window on the roof, sir." I didn't want to say more than I needed to, I'd been brought back to the reality that I could still be sent to prison. He looked back up at me as he finished wrapping my hands.

"And what brought you to be on that roof in the first place, Johnny?"

"I-I was just climbing, sir."

"Just climbing?"

"Y-yes sir, I'd been wanting to practice, and had chosen this one on account of its height, I just didn't expect to fall through." I laughed, making light of the situation, he didn't.

"You don't think I'm a fool, but you must think you're a far better liar than you are." He responded, to my shock. "I know who you are, Johnny Bull, or would you prefer *Garrath*?"

"I-, h-how do you know my name?"

He smiled and walked me over to what I assumed was his office, where he revealed a small picture of my family by a pile of envelopes.

"The man who approached me, whom I mentioned in my speech, that was your father, Garrath. He's told me much about you. He's worried for you, your mother, and his country."

"Does he know what I've been doing?"

"Oh, no. I pieced that together myself: A boy your age, climbing buildings, with an ear for my message, and a background such as yours, it was a fair guess."

"Sir, I don't want to go to jail-"

"Your secret is safe with me, Garrath. Where politics fail, men of action must do what is necessary to protect that which they love, it is the natural drive of men to preserve that which they hold sacred."

I felt inspired, a wave of relief washed over me.

"You should campaign for Prime Minister." I told him. "We need someone like you who is willing to listen to our situation, someone who cares."

"After that speech, my boy, I don't believe it's likely I'll be granted campaign for anything." He answered.

"You said it yourself, you spoke the thoughts of the silent majority. We only need for a politician to stand up with us, we whose voices are confined by stigma."
I reached my hand out to him.
"You don't have the right not to do so." I told him. His expression changed from a disheartened pout to an encouraged grin.

California, Berkeley
June 25 1969
|Mister Doctor|

Since we lost the commander, the party has fractured; it splintered into a few groups, none of which quite held the power of the united party.

The militia remained grossly loyal to me, a force of some six hundred disciplined, trained, and armed men, although a portion of our stormtroopers had seemingly vanished. My concerns were piqued when it seemed one of our caches had been entirely looted; I responded by dispatching my own men to regather what we had in the lower New England region.

Despite minor fallbacks, as far as the power of the party that remained, I feel the greater heft of it stuck with us.

The few moments I didn't grind away preserving and promoting the party, I spent rifling through the commanders records to pin down his assassin. The police had turned up empty handed, giving up so quickly as to not waste time on a *'worthless racist'*. We know it was someone on the inside, it just became too difficult to track everyone after the group's splintering. I will find him, in time, but right now the survival of the party was what mattered most.

Internally we were soldiers, we'd hone our abilities, put them to the test, organize operations for dissemination of propaganda, but on the surface we cloaked our project as a patriotic self-improvement program; *'Get fit, Get strong, Find your future'* was our slogan; a slogan touted out by our *white-shirts* to the high-school and college boys before subversive teachings could have the chance to corrupt their impressionable minds.

We weren't looking to force or coerce, you don't gain loyalty that way, only compliance; no, we'd just give these boys the proper guidance to think clearly and act swiftly, if then they continue on to join the party is entirely their choice, which is precisely what we need; loyalty.

To the public we were the Minutemen Association, or just Minutemen for short, a group who in their free time would organize sporting events, and gave lectures on the importance of hard work, strength and loyalty to fatherland.

We'd successfully established branches all across the country, and were completing our tour in Berkeley, California, where exactly one year ago the Commander and I were doing precisely this same routine: Recruiting for the party.

While I may not be able to prevent the catastrophe we saw on the horizon, the Commander may be proud that we'll be prepared for it, and America will live on.

"-Gentlemen, there is no argument about the fact that we live in a deeply troubled society, I believe most of you will agree with that." I spoke to the audience of college students. To my words some nodded and mumbled amongst themselves.
"Where we disagree is plainly which aspects of society are indeed the troubled ones; there's a seeming political polarization as to what is right and what is wrong, when in fact the ideologies of both sides have been poisoned and corrupted, leaving the average everyman to choose between two routes to the same destination, and that destination is exploitation, be it of the communist variety or of the cronyist capital variety. There is an alternative. Let me tell you that we as humans can learn best from the natural world that we so often forget we are a part of. Nature has ingrained a set of principles within us which throughout time and history, religion and morals have attempted to encapsulate and codify, but we've strayed far from god and moral principle. Science has granted us a third opportunity to reconnect with natural law, and it is through it that we can salvage the teachings of faith and philosophy to properly meet certain biological truths and the needs of people today. One of the fundamental yet seemingly most controversial of these truths is that of race, of human distinction and variation, as well as plain incompatibility in a multicultural society. Darwin once said, *when two organisms occupy the same niche there will be competition*, and that truth grows exponentially when you apply it to those of different tribes and wholly different peoples. Now this does not mean I am seeking to persecute or harm any man on account of his race, he can't help what race he is! Simply, we believe the races **are** incontestably distinct, a distinction which is more than skin deep! Are you to tell me we've become externally so distinct through adaptation, yet our brains, the most complex organ in our bodies, remained absolutely the same across thousands of years and thousands of miles of adaptation? I consider myself a scientifically

inclined man, science and history were great interests of mine in youth, and one of the most remarkable things about our reality is a little process called evolution, that animals adapt to be better suited for survival in their environments, and that you can breed better or worse animals, yet somehow we are told it is immoral to apply this same scientific principle to the races of man. We are after all biological creatures like the animals around us, and like animals, humans are forced to abide by the same natural laws of this world, but '*no*' says your professors, *humans, distinct from animals, are all equal*, they'll say. What explanation is there for this? There is none, they shrug off evolution the moment it no longer serves as a useful tool to them, and that's because if you're honest about evolution, on a long enough timeline, it's downright impossible not to become what these liberals deem a "Nazi". We believe in the natural roles of men and women, we believe in our distinction from other races through the natural process of evolution, we believe in the honesty of reality, in what is true. The divide ought not be between right-wing and left-wing, but those who believe in the ways of nature, and those of the unnatural world who risk plunging us into animalistic chaos. We are at the mercy of nature, but unlike petty animals, have been gifted the ability to consciously act in harmony with it! The *unnaturals* will acknowledge we are animals, yet encourage us to believe we are gods, a belief that will surely drive us backward into a state of disharmonious savagery. We who believe in the natural order advocate humble virtue, to recognize our nature as mere parts of this natural world, yet never cease in our drive to become better humans, to champion the values of discipline, of decency, the values which make men good fathers, and women good mothers, roles which are increasingly being diminished in favor of hedonistic pleasure with no thought for the future implications; truly the indulgent, non-reflective lifestyle of an arrogant beast. I fear the loss of the socio-biological system which has made us a strong, hardy, innovative, daring, and freedom-loving people, the same system that has made our nation a healthy body where every part functions just as it should."

I took a momentary pause which some of the audience misinterpreted as a conclusion, and believed called for applause. I continued,

"I am not a college man; my teenage years were spent in Vietnam fighting a war I was told would protect my country. I've known what it is like to face the brutality and cruelty of combat. What in dire, real situations is necessary to survive. You, on the other hand, were sent here, most of you paid for by your parents, to substitute experience for the information a biased, liberal professor tells you is truth. Many of you perhaps have never fired a gun, or been in a fight, or hunted your own food." I glanced around the room. "-never built anything that you can call yours, repaired a complex device, or even so much as risked your skin for something truly worthwhile. These things I'm listing may sound arbitrary, but to a man these can be some of the most important and most valuable lessons you will ever learn, they will open a new perspective to you which you can choose to follow down a path toward what nature truly recognizes as a man, one who can think free of distraction, who can survive on his own accord, and take necessary action when needed."
My assistants began handing out pamphlets for our association.
"If you're daring enough to see things from the other side, memberships are open to all willing participants. Details will be in the pamphlets distributed, thank you very much."

The audience applauded, some remained silent and skeptical, and several others still booed and heckled. These students have become more intolerant to new ideas in only the past year, or perhaps I'm still not quite the speaker that the Commander was.

As I prepared to exit to meet with my men, I was cut off by a protest party, a title perhaps too generous for this gang of thugs clad in black and carrying with them blunt objects. They shouted at me in the halls, yelling "*Nazi go home!*". They'd cut me off, and were seemingly attempting to corner me. Thinking on my feet, I dashed into the staircase, making my way to another floor, I'd been so caught up in avoiding the crowd that I didn't pay attention to where I was walking.

As I turned a corner, hoping to find an exit, I walked right into someone else, a professor it seemed. I'd knocked him over.

"I'm sorry about that, I wasn't looking where I was going." I said offering a hand up. He remained silent, glaring at me. He'd dropped a number of papers which he began gathering off the floor. I lent a hand.
"I hope you're not gravely upset, it was an accident." I handed him his papers, and after a long minute of silence, he finally spoke.

"It's alright." He said in a soft nasally voice. "I wasn't paying much attention myself. Preoccupied with these-" He crumpled a piece of paper. "-work assignments."

"Difficult work?" I asked him as we began walking together, assuming he could lead me back to the main hall.

"Precisely the opposite, simple work. The answers are quite plainly in the textbook if you invest the effort to look for it, but I've been hard-pressed to find a student with the slightest iota of investment in the subject, so I'm forced to review this monkey scratch as a formality, knowing full well that not a single one will be a demonstrator of competence." He responded.

"What subject do you teach?" I asked, slipping a paper from his folder.

"Advanced mathematics, Calculus specifically."

"Not my forte, unfortunately." I handed the workslip back. "My name's Doctor, by the way, Augustus Doctor." I held out my hand for a handshake.

"Theodore." He said as he shook my hand.

"Can I call you Ted?"

"Yes, you may." We'd reached his office. "You're that men's empowerment speaker, are you not?"

"Well yes, that would be me." I answered.

He turned slowly from the door, avoiding eye contact with me, and reminding me that he had avoided looking me in the eyes during our entire walk.

"You have a history with that US Nazi Party, do you not?" He said as if he was gearing up for a long line of questioning.

"Yes sir, I was a close friend of the Commander." I answered.

"Yes, that Commander had given speeches here before, I caught a few in my spare time; while I can't agree with every aspect of the ideology, I'm not deeply familiar with it myself, I would say-" He stepped closer and finally looked me in the eyes. "-we may share some common ground." He stepped back, and opened his door. "Step inside, I believe you and I can share an intelligent conversation that'll give me an escape from this cage of mental density."

I took a seat down on a couch while he sat across from me, tossing his papers into the waste bin. Our '*conversation*' amounted to him rambling to me near nonstop, the only time I'd speak would be when he'd intentionally pause to allow me to ask a question.

"-I can no longer tolerate this hyper sensitive environment." He continued. "I am tired of the pampered, entitled attitudes these ignoramuses bring to my classes, their belief that I, and the class too, are obligated to appeal to their social sensibilities. Mathematics aren't a football game or a nightclub. They expect me to pass and excuse their shoddiness. There's no discipline, no seriousness, no ethic for hard work! If they don't understand a subject, do they try harder? No. They expect the system to allow them to slide through the cracks because the system doesn't want thinkers, it wants workers, mindless drones. I refuse to be a gear in such a machine." Ted ranted.

"And how do you feel this correlates with our stance on America?" I asked.

"Because we recognize two aspects of the same disease; these same slackers that the universities churn out hate America's strength, specifically white, male America, white-male Americans and their success. Why? Because the slacker suffers from a subconscious realization that they are inferior. The slacker hates strength, individualism, confidence, masculinity, and achievement because it forces him to contrast it with himself, to face the truth; that he is a loser."

Ted stumbled up from his chair to his desk where he grasped a portfolio.

"Their culture is probably best characterized as that of a dying society, almost suicidal, saturated in defeatism. This culture of despair resonates with what they recognize as a reflection of their inner selves. Alternatively, they seek oversaturation of hedonism, sexuality, perversity, and escapism to drown out their realities and perceptions of the future with momentary, immediate sensations of gratification, so never must they face the ugly truth, the unhappy truth that they will fail unless they become like the thing they've learned to hate more every single day: Strong. Hard-working. Resolute. Disciplined. But the world around them discourages it, and for good reason; If the slacker refuses to become a strong, rather, a ***truly*** strong individual, then his only means of strength exists in the collective, only with his fellow slackers; only as an angry mass does strength exist among them, an angry mass to be controlled and organized by the very same professors and philosophers who instill these values into them!"

"Marxists." I responded.

"Leftists, I'd say. Members of the ideological left, be they communists or liberals, they share a common trait of self-hatred to some degree, of inferiority to the bourgeois or the privileged of society for having something they don't, I've seen this insanity go as far as a desire to augment their weak bodies with machinery, it's down right sickening. Sometimes I wish we'd actually pursued the space missions as planned, instead of this so called '*Tech Revolution*'. Bah." He expressed his disgust. "Nature has gifted us a form which we can hone to tremendous heights, and yet here is a surrender to that which is easy and new, that which alleviates the pain of responsibility and individual strength." He sunk back into his chair.
"We are spiraling into a society of soulless, medically-sedated human cogs whose sole purpose will be to power a machine that thinks and acts for us, we'll merely serve our purpose and drown ourselves in the hollowest of pleasures, becoming grey shadows of what was once known as an independent, unique human-being. I can't tolerate it anymore, neither the environment, nor being a tool of the system. I like you, Mister Doctor, because you stand in pure opposition to the degenerative leftists. You are a pillar of what, I'm sure many would contest, but to me, is the voice of order, of individuality, of fortitude; the cohesive force to unite the disintegrating nation, if there is indeed hope of saving it." He ran his hand across his forehead. "I myself, I just need to get away from it. Our skill sets are not identical, and I cannot lead the same crusade you do. I only wish there was something I could do to help you."

"You can help us by helping yourself. *We* are America. Learn more, grow more, and when the day comes, protect what you stand for." I answered.

"Precisely, Doctor. The only strength that I possess is the strength that *I* possess. I've greatly appreciated speaking with you, sir. I hope our paths cross again someday." Ted smiled and walked me to the door. Before I left I asked him,

"How do you believe you'll change things, Ted?" I lost his eye contact.

"You are a cohesive force, Doctor, a uniter. Something needs to fall apart before if can be put back together." He returned eye contact. "I'll help crack the glass for you."

Texas, Kirk Ranch
July 4 1970
|Del Kirk|

"*-I'm deeply saddened by this turn of events; the continued agitation of our nation by the state of Texas, especially on this celebration of our independence. We shall not tolerate these aggressions, and thus I have authorized the beginning of military action to bring the rogue state of Texas back into the Union.*" The President was making another announcement on the T.V.
"*The law abiding need not fear any repercussions, simply remain at home, and under no circumstances involve yourselves with the insurgent forces of Del Kirk.*"

"That sonva'bitch!" Pops shouted as he burst in through the door. "We've gotta move on out quick, junior! We don't have a lot of time!"

"Pops, what happened?" I asked.

"We stood our ground, son, that's what happened. There was a gun raid on the town hall, 'tried to take our stockpile, but we stood our ground and we're gonna keep standing our ground, boy. It's our lives or our way of life, and I ain't given to parting with either or." Pops pulled out his gun cases from behind the wall panels, and carried them out to the truck. Ever since that knock on our door, pop has been preparing for catastrophe, suiting up the truck with thicker wheels and metal plating, it was a darn military vehicle by this point. "Junior! Get your mother, we're not safe here no more! Shannon! Grab our valuables and meet me in the truck! We've got to get a move on!"

I rushed to my room to grab my revolver, Ma was gathering our clothes and silver in a suitcase. We dashed down the stairs and out to the truck where pops was speaking with some of our neighbors; Mr.Houston, Uncle Stark, and Mr.Hughes.

"You're goin' somewhere safe, junior. The time has come for your pops to take a stand for the country just like our founders did. It's pretty exciting, huh?" He said kneeling down to my level, trying to make light of what I knew was an uncertain situation. He could tell I was worried by my silence. "You got your gun, Junior? Still remember how to use it?" I nodded, he nodded back.

Pop led me and ma into the truck.

"I'm bringin' you two somewhere safe." Pop said as he started the engine, and drove us away. "I've got no idea how long this is gonna last, but I've got to be out there as long as it does. I'll drop by every chance I can. Junior, you with that gun are the last line of defense should something go down when I'm not around. Keep your ma safe, and remember, the lord is with you, always."

England, Birmingham
August 5 1970
|Garrath King|

It'd been a right glorious few months, it has.
Gates of Vienna had become the talk of the land. Not a newsstand, not a voice, not a mind neglected to pay it some attention.
The controversy of so high-ranking a politician to speak out on such a scandalous matter was too savory for the vulturous news parasites to not lap-up; of course they put their spin on the story, infused every word they wrote with double-entendre, and hidden meaning they expected us to unconsciously register as the true narrative, but the people couldn't deny what they felt deep in the hearts of themselves;

Our home was under invasion, hidden only in passive form, but that passivity disappeared the moment you brought up the prospect of deportation or of English right to this land.

"What even is an englishman?" They'd ask as if it were some trivial question, that to be English was little but a fashionable item to be handed out.
We knew well who we were and what we wanted, we just needed a man with the courage and influence to speak the thoughts we all shared.

Gates of Vienna inflamed a blaze of national passion and zeal that burned the blinds pulled over our eyes, and set us free to move forward with full force.

The Pakis and Asians didn't take much kindly to English love of English land, they rallied against us, citing hate and discrimination as grounds to outlaw our voices, and the establishment for the most part enabled them!

We were determined to put **OUR** politicians in power, to restore true democracy of the people in place of this illusion we've been sold as truth.

Political action alone would not suffice, I did believe, sometimes it is necessary to act out, to demonstrate that our words hold weight, that they are not merely words, but a prophecy to be fulfilled should conditions be met.

I had organized with the community of Birmingham for the prosecution of a grooming gang, immigrant men who have preyed on young English girls, and long gone unpunished by the paralyzed system.

Today was to be the day of their conviction and if the court would not convict, we would.

For eight hours we stood surrounding the courthouse and only upon the opening of the doors did we learn a conviction was not brought.

The rapists were protected by armored officers, officers who attempted to disburse and beat us back, we whose land and people have been defiled by these invaders.

They assumed we were all talk, that we were domesticated enough to not bite the hand of big government, that we were too fearful and weak to take matters into our own hands. I gave my word to bring justice and I would.

I stood out of the crowd, and approached as close as the guards would allow before warning me to stop. I was not domesticated as they were, so I stepped forward for one officer to beat me down. I refused to relent, and attempted further until one raised a gun toward me, but a man from our crowd placed a hand on his shoulder, giving him a disapproving nod, encouraging him to lower his weapon.

One by one, young men from the crowd stepped forward to stand by me, raising me from the floor.

Massachusetts, Rockport Town
September 12, 1970
|Percy Holiday|

"-Former member of the United States Nazi Party, and now leader of the rising *New Amerika Movement*, Mister Augustus Doctor, had this to say,"

"Mister President, we the American people, the silent majority, speak today through one voice; Your tyranny is no longer tolerated. From the shores of New Dixie, to the Free States of Arizona, Utah, New Mexico and Texas. A great warning alarm should be sounding in your head: Resign. End this catastrophe before it starts. More states will break away, and you can rest assured that the American people

will support them in their quest of independence from your socialistic, subversive regime-!"

It was another foggy night, mom was watching the news, the room was full of smoke, and I couldn't wait to get outside.

I'd slipped on my rain-boots, and tossed on a new coat.

"Mom! I'm stepping out!"

She told me not to get into any trouble.
"*-It's the last thing I need right now*." She ended with.

It felt rougher with her every year, like she hated me, or thought of me as an unwelcome guest, I really felt it too. I'd try to spend as little time at home as possible, and since I met my new friends, home's really just been a place to sleep and wake up.

"Hey there, bud." Holden said, slapping me on the back as I came down the stairs.

"How's it going, kid, you wanna smoke?" Tyler asked, Holden scolding him. "What?" He asked Holden coyly.

"He's a kid!" Holden said through gritted teeth.

"I'm a kid." Tyler shot back.

"No thanks, I don't like smoke." I said.

"See, man, the kid can speak for himself!" Tyler said antagonistically.

"Don't test me, Ty, you know I'll kick your ass."

"A'right, a'right."

"I ain't kidding, man."

"You wanna go? Right outside the kid's door? While he's right here?"

"Perc, you have any problem watching a fight?" Holden asked, putting a hand on my shoulder.
I nodded *no*, and just a second after, Holden delivered an uppercut to Tyler's ribs, leaving him stumbling, and clumsily grabbing Holden's arm while punching him in the back.
Holden was winning the fight pretty squarely, but Tyler did pull off some tricks, kicking Holden off of him when they had fallen on the ground, and getting him in a headlock before Holden reversed it on him, forcing him to tap out, and collapse on the floor.
"Not bad, man." Holden said panting, offering Tyler a hand.

"What'd you think, kid?" Tyler asked me.

"That was pretty cool." I said grinning.

"Yeah? You know, when you're older, we're not gonna hold back on you."

"I ain't fightin' him." Holden scolded.

"***I'm*** not gonna hold back on you." Tyler said laughing, gently punching my shoulder.
"Alright, so what's on the agenda for today?"

"Today-" Holden started. "-we're goin' underground."

"You mean what I think you mean?" Tyler asked with excitement.

"What're you guys talking about?" I asked.

"May be better if I just showed you what I mean." Holden guided us into an alley where he lifted up a sewer grate and started climbing

down. "Come on, Percy! Water's just fine!" I climbed down, Tyler followed after me.
"Being so close to the coast, the town's sewer system is built with access to nearly every municipal building, you know, for utility purposes, and that includes Town Hall."

"What's at town hall?" I asked again.

"Well, uh, nothin' really, I just thought it'd be cool to snoop around. Now, thing is-" Holden got back to his narrating. "-to keep thieves out, they've either cemented or bricked up these old access doors, but Tyler and I've been at it trying to open them back up. Tyler, can you go grab our sledge? I think we left it on one of the gates between fifth and fourth street."

"Aye aye, captain!" Tyler joked before taking off.

"We'll meet yah at city hall! Don't get lost!" Holden yelled out.

We walked about fifteen minutes, splashing through sewer water before we reached the entrance we were looking for, it was bricked up alright, with a good lot of cracks in it from what I assumed were past visits from Tyler and Holden.

"She just needs a few more well placed hits, 'n we'll have total access to the place."

"Do you think anyone will notice the bricks are gone?" I asked.

"No, I-I don't think so; no one ever comes down here, let alone to this corner of the sewer. Besides, we'll toss the broken bricks into the running water so the current'll carry them off. Nobody'll notice any difference." Just then I heard Tyler splashing toward us.

"Found it!" He called out, bringing Holden the sledge hammer

.

"Alright fellas, no going back now. You might want to step back a few feet though."

As we did, Holden took to the bricks with swing after swing until the door was cleared. There was a lock on it, but Holden gave that a hefty swing too, and it came right off.

"Percy, would you like to have the honor of being the first boy to set foot in town hall after dark?"

"Damn right I would!" I walked forward when Holden told me to watch the cussing before letting me step in, they followed close behind.

We were in awe of how big the place looked while it was empty, the dark only made the walls look ever taller, and further away.

Tyler climbed up onto the stage, and began making as if he was giving mayoral announcements while Holden and I walked around, checking behind every door, looking for something of interest.

"Find anything cool, Percy?"

"Not yet, just offices it looks like."

"You know, fellas, we ought to do stuff like this more often." Tyler said taking a seat on the corner of the stage.

"Yeah, we should." Holden responded.

"No, I really mean it, we ought-to do something like this every week, but maybe bigger, think, maybe, Boston, huh? Roadtrip get anyone excited?"

"I don't drive, you drive?" Holden challenged Tylers idea.

"No, but I mean, we will pretty soon, we're only getting older, Percy too! I mean it, do you wanna look back at these years, and say '*yeah I hung around Rockport with my friends, we broke into town hall once, but that's really it*'." Tyler spoke mockingly. "When I'm old, I wanna say '*Fuck yeah! I pushed the limits, I broke the law, I had a damn good time!*', I mean, don't you? Hell, we'll never be this young again, man. Right now, this is our youth, this is the youngest we'll ever be; we can't move back, we can't save it for later, we gotta make it count!"

"Sounds like you're having a midlife crisis." Holden mocked.

"Maybe I am, man! I been watching the news, man, some scary stuff's happening; you heard the governments building robots now!? I don't know. This shit's too damn crazy, maybe it ain't real, or maybe the damn world could end tomorrow. You guys are my best friends, everyone else is so fuckin' out of it, they rather bum around a city than do shit like this! You know, real experience, something that makes me a little scared, but I don't care 'cause I'm with my best buds. I know you feel it too, man, this here-" Tyler slammed his hand on the wooden stage. "-this is real. I wanna climb buildings, man. I wanna see wild forests, and chicks changing in a college locker room, stuff everyone wants to do but never does!"

Holden looked at me, nodding.
"The world's changing, might not be this fun forever. Might never get chances like these again. Fuck it, sounds like a plan, man." Holden responded.

"Hell yeah, man! What about you, kid?" Tyler asked me.

"Damn right! Yeah!"

"I said watch the cussing, Percy." Holden told me.

"Yeah, do as we say, not as we do." Tyler added, I laughed. It started to feel like the beginning of something great.

Chapter 3
London England, Recording Studio
October 14 1970
|Garrath King|

"-Today I would like to introduce a very unique guest, one I'd wager you wouldn't expect to broadcast his identity to the country in such a manner. He is a political activist, a modern day Robin Hood, a criminal to some, and few may even dare to call him a gang leader; ladies and gentlemen I am pleased to introduce, Johnny Bull." The announcer paused to allow the sound of applause to play. "Now the matter of your true name, it is public in the record; however, I understand you'd prefer not to mention it to a broad audience."

"Yes, yes, frankly I'm not ashamed to let the public know who I am, my purpose in concealing my identity had been to avoid incarceration; however, thanks to a pardoning by our new prime minister, I've been free to come out, and wear my title proudly. My current concern is for my family, whom I would not want to put at risk of harassment." I spoke into the microphone.

"Now the pardoning of the prime minister, do you feel that was a moral decision? I-I'm sure you do-" He laughed. "-Rather, do you believe it was within reasonable legal bounds. Not to be brash, but the activities you participated in were certainly of a criminal nature: Thievery, assault, property damage to name a few." He asked.

"This was all well investigated by the proper authorities, and I can tell you personally that I only targeted those of a criminal background, men and families I had known to be exploiting our financial system, participating in smuggling, distribution of illicit substances, and much worse. Criminals deserve reprisal, yet no one would act, therefore I was forced to take law enforcement into my own hands."

"And that does not make you a criminal, in your opinion?" The host asked me.

"In mine and that of the just law. Five years ago I could well have been imprisoned for so much as an insistence that an immigrant had been participating in illegal activity, the crime of prejudice, of stereotyping, what reason is there to that? England was asleep while its home was ransacked, I simply fended off the intruder until England woke up."

The host flipped through a number of cue cards with questions on them before he asked,

"You've seemingly done well to transform your Johnny Bull political identity into something of a business or organization; however, some would argue this association is little more than a gang of thugs with direct financial support from the public, how do you respond?"

"The Bulldogs are a pro-Fatherland activist group whose purpose is simply to identify and expose illegal migrant activity, and take the actions necessary to bring these criminals to justice or expel them from England if necessary. It is true that some of our boys partake in violent activity which I do not condone; however, they have free agency, and I thus cannot be responsible for the actions of some bad apples in the bunch; membership is as simple as pledging allegiance to England, the Bulldogs, and wearing the uniform, I can't exactly revoke ones membership by simply taking away a card or scratching a name off a list."

"And of the money you receive?" He asked. "It's clear the public supports you generously, certainly enough to open up your own establishment, which to me seems like a clubhouse operated out of a tavern. Does this seem like a responsible use of public money?"

"Donations to the Bulldogs go toward the benefit of myself, the group, and to the English people. Understand that being who I am, it isn't easy to hold a regular job without the risk of harassment or outright termination; therefore, funds are clearly allocated to help me support a modest lifestyle. I will admit; however, there was one time I indulged myself in a luxury item; I purchased for myself and for my father a pair of exquisite matching cars; we'd been forced to take public transport after the bank repossessed my fathers vehicle years ago, I promised him that one day I would get it back, with interest. As for our so called '*clubhouse*', it's a place of organization and to attract new members. We hold beerhall discussions every week, and plan community outreach as would be done in any public-betterment organization such as ours."

"Very good. It's been a pleasure having you on the show, Mr.Bull. To our audience, stay tuned for our next segment on *the rising dilemma of invasive technology in daily life, and why it may just save yours.*" The host thanked me as he wrapped up the segment.

"The pleasure's been all mine."

England, Birmingham
December 18 1970
|Mister Doctor|

I took a trip abroad to meet with some of the Commander's former overseas connections, I was looking to muster a bit of international support from Canada, Ireland, and the UK to help give my movement back home greater legitimacy, but most of them were uninterested in what I was offering. A lot of big talk it seemed, but little action.

While I was in Britain, I managed to arrange a meeting with the newly elected Prime Minister, he was a nationalist it seemed, 'became fairly popular after his *Gates of Vienna* speech.

I reached out to him by phone only to discover he'd heard of me and wanted to speak the very next day.

"I'd very much like to congratulate you on your victory, Mr.Prime Minister. Your campaign has been inspiring to many nationalists both here and abroad, myself included."

"That's very kind of you, Mister Doctor." He said. "I had debated if in fact I should campaign at all, but granted the damning calls to action, I did not feel I had the right not to declare my candidacy, and speak for those whose voices had been hushed silent. I hear you too may be sensing the call to action as well."

"Our current administration has proven itself incapable and unfavorable to lead. A movement is being pushed forward to impeach current leadership from office legally, though the *Amerikan* people are willing to take matters into their own hands if necessary."

"Yes." He agreed. "A more hands on approach seems to be your strong suit."

"Which is in part why I have made this trip here, I understand that you alone are not what is driving Britain in the direction of national consciousness, there is the matter of *Johnny Bull*, I believe some claim he was once a criminal."

"A vigilante, one acting on behalf of the English population when the government would not act to protect its own people. His actions have been pardoned, those he'd stolen from were not merely targeted for their race. Money launderers, smugglers, drug dealers, yes, all immigrants, but these men that Johnny took a stand against were, because of their immigration status, a protected class, a privileged class which to even attribute such crimes to could have been considered discrimination. I do not and never will approve of bringing harm to an innocent individual, regardless of his background, but incontestably it is clear that Johnny was targeting criminal types."

"He does seem to have a strong sense of justice." I withdrew from my briefcase a file, and handed it to the Prime Minister. "I've been studying Johnny very closely, and would like to speak with him personally."

"It won't be difficult to find him." The Prime Minister took a pen and paper, writing and handing me an address.

I followed the directions to come upon what resembled a tavern of sorts, the windows barred, the door made of metal, the sign overhead reading '*The Bulldogs*'.

This was where Johnny Bull spent his time. Apparently his popularity brought him a loyal following, his so called *vanguard* against the immigrant menace that infested his streets. They were a boorish lot of young hoodlums in black hoods who cracked up other hoodlums. I saw them, bodies covered in grotesque tattoos, funneling alcohol down their throats, swearing and whooping to a soccer game playing on the televisions of the bar. I saw little difference between them and a common gang.

I stood out like a sore thumb, clad in a maroon suit and white shirt contrasting heavily with every occupant of the bar, they dressed in black coats with a Union Jack smearly painted on their backs.

"'Got a problem, mate?" One asked me.

"I need to speak with Bull."

"Who's asking?"

"The Prime Minister sent me." I answered, my response met with skeptical glances, but the fella in front of me could tell I was serious.

"'Pologies, right this way, sir." He led me past a stage to an office area behind the tavern, bringing me to a door with '*Johnny*' printed on the window.

"He's right in 'ere. Give it a knock 'fore you enter." He walked off, I knocked and let myself in.

"Mr.Bull." I called.

"I don't like to be disturbed." He said looking down at a map of the city.

"-Perhaps a tavern wasn't the best choice for an office, then. My name's Doctor, Mister Doctor."

"'Right, what can I do you for?" He looked up, pushing the map aside. "Having a little migrant dilemma?"

"Not quite. As you might be able to tell, I'm not from here."

"Yeah, thought you sounded American." He pointed out obviously.

"Right. You may not keep up with American politics, but I'm the head of a group similar to yours, a militia party who's looking to clean up the country."

"Mmhmm." He went, scratching at some stubble on his chin.

"We have an official membership of some ten thousand armed, trained men in New England alone." This caught his attention. "That's not even counting our independent reserve supporters who may well number near a million."

"So you're pretty big then?" Bull crossed his arms and listened.

"Yes, but you see, I came here because I'm seeking to establish a nationalist alliance between my men in the US, and the British government for immediate recognition of us and other approved secessionist movements once we have assumed power in the region of Greater New England. We already have the Prime Minister's support." Bull shifted around his seat, and leaned forward.

"In that case, what is it you want from me?"

"Spoken support is good for official politics, but the world needs to know this change is real, thus I want your support and the support of your men on American soil, to let the world know the severity of this situation."

"N-Now hold on, why us? If the prime minister supports you, why not just send in the royal navy-?" Bull stammered.

"This is grassroots, just like what you did here; you took action, and the politicians followed. Politicians can say all they want, but the people need to know they hold the power. I want to provide your men with proper training, because what you have out there, these are not soldiers, these are not proper role models for the law-abiding, these are hoodlums, many I'm sure are no better than the immigrants they expel. Am I wrong? They ought be better than the immigrants, right? There's hardly an ounce of discipline between everyone in that room, but a bounty of loyalty; loyalty to you, they will follow you, they are nothing but a tribe, and you are their chief. Be an example to them, be a leader worthy of following, lead your tribe to become an empire." As I finished my dialogue, Bull relaxed, slumping back in his chair.

"Where do I begin?"

"Tomorrow, you will call a meeting, tolerate not the slightest bit of rowdiness; someone speaks, shut them up, someone fidgets, berate them. Show them that it's time to begin acting like men, that now is the time to focus their actions into a fine-point that will cut the parasites from Britain's body with surgical precision, and those who can't function within this new order will be dismissed. There can be no room for sloppiness or disloyalty. This is the beginning of a new order, and order cannot exist without men willing to enforce and follow it. Is that understood, Bull?"

"Yes, sir."

I took a step back, realizing I was speaking to someone much like myself, just a young man, the same young man who enlisted to fight in 'Nam; eager, angry, I saw an opportunity.

"How old are you?" I asked.

"Twenty, sir." Bull responded.

"I'm not much older than you. Have you served in the military?"

"No, sir. I always wanted to."

"It changes the way you see things. A tough life has helped harden you into becoming a man, but you're not quite there yet, still reckless, still driven by directionless anger, but what if I told you that I could help you be the man England needs you to be? It won't be easy, you may grow to hate it, but it will make you stronger than you could ever imagine, and when you return home, you'll be ready to make the changes that need to be made. You're going to need practice, and there's no better learning experience than the real thing. You're going to war, Bull."

New York, Kingston New Amerika Compound II
December 14 1973
|Garrath King|

Mister Doctor has taken us well under his wing of military training, most of us hadn't even held a gun prior, but he ensured we were well accustomed to the weapons soon upon our arrival. He was well respected in these parts of the states, New England and Northern

New York, that is; it allowed his men to stockpile weapons freely even following the nationwide restrictions. Most around these Northern states were strong adherents to their right to arms regardless, only increasing the ease with which we operated free of federal jurisdiction.

Our original stronghold, where we all would train, where we slept, stored our supplies and arms was the New Amerika Compound in New Hampshire, it was a fine installation settled on a plot of some ten acres of land.

Doctor did as he promised, and made of us a capable army, formidable even. He encouraged me to instruct my men on my own tactical skills: Scaling, infiltration, and the like; I was delighted to pass on these skills, and in essence create a legion of Johnny Bulls, it's what I'd hoped we could have been from the very beginning.

We'd developed a strong reputation in New England, or rather Doctor had. The government certainly was stepping far out of bounds, trodding heavily and carelessly atop the freedoms I expected to be held so dear. Many counties opted for our personal protection and for the commandeering of their national guard personnel to serve exclusively as a New England army.

Eventually our luck ran out; the federal government decided we'd grown large enough to actually make a difference, and thus posed a threat to their order, no doubt spying on us via some secret surveillance technology locals have spoken whispers of.

The government dispatched it's cronies to come kick in our doors, prepared with a warrant for Doctor's arrest, and the confiscation of our possessions. Surely we wouldn't allow it, and a firefight ensued.

This was the first time I was forced to take up a gun against another man, but I was never one to stand down when my brothers were under threat, and that was what the Doctor had become to me, that is what my fellow soldiers were to me. We needed Doctor, and he needed us.

We would not let them take him.

Our great numbers within our own compound gave us a sheer advantage, and it was clear that those agents were nervous serving these demands upon us. Doctor resisted, they prepared to act with force, we made our preemptive strike upon them, whittling their numbers to none within a matter of minutes, but this only brought down fire upon us.

Outside our compound laid in wait an army of reinforcements, of tanks, of helicopters, and of countless armored men prepared to siege our fortifications.

We barricaded the entrances, and prepared for the hell to come. Doctor took to the loudspeaker, making a call for peace, reminding these men that this would only end with bloodshed for both sides, expressing only the desire to be left alone.

There was a brief quiet afterward, a torturous anxiety and uncertainty that left our trigger fingers shaking.

As much as we hoped it would miraculously end there, we knew well it wouldn't; the jolting awakening came in the form of cracking machine gun fire.

We lost dozens of men over the course of two weeks.

They attacked brutally and relentlessly. As a group of men without women or children among us, they held back little, and spared no cruelty in attempting to coerce a surrender.

There were times I myself wanted to give up, where the fear nearly consumed me to the point of desiring a swift death, but Doctor encouraged me to fight on. Our resources weren't yet gone, if I gave up now, I'd be surrendering not only myself, but all of my men to these bastards. I wouldn't have it.

In our darkest moments of the third week, as our ammunition hit dangerous lows, and food rations shrunk to minuscule portions, the fire finally stopped. The soldiers retreated from our lands, and we couldn't understand why.

It wouldn't be until the next day that we heard of what happened, the president, *the tyrant*, had been assassinated. An explosion had devastated his office, and his successors had called off the assault. It was a miracle for us.

Approaching Doctor on his opinion of the matter, he only spoke cryptically.

"The glass is cracking. It's time to hammer in the last blows. We're going to need a major restock of our ammunition, and some heavier gunpower."

Right then I wasn't sure what he was referring to, but restock we did. We built an even larger compound here in the city of Kingston, here where we now housed armored vehicles, helicopters, and mobile artillery. It became clear we were gearing up for total war.

Texas, Kirk Ranch
July 4 1974
|Del Kirk|

I gently strummed my guitar, concluding a hymn. I held up the picture of my parents.
"Hope you two are lookin' over me."
I gave the picture a kiss and safely set it by my mementos above the empty fireplace.

"-this very grim fourth of July marks the fourth anniversary of Bloody Texas, the eighth year of the nationwide race riots which began here in L.A, Detroit, Chicago, New York, and New Orleans. Seven months since the assassination of the President in an explosion which devastated the white house, and the Sustainable Government Protocol was initiated in the remaining Union. I think we can all agree it's time we reconsider what Independence Day means to us as Americ-"

The damn radio's no source for entertainment these days.

I stepped along the creaking wood floor to the kitchen. The farms have been lucky enough to remain in good supply thanks to water recycling; no one's gone hungry, though some have gone thirsty. I could use a little drink myself.

Those damn feds had taken my father from me; ma didn't last long after without pop around, eventually just leaving me with nothing but my thoughts and the bible for a time.
I really felt like god was punishing me for the longest time; it took that time to realize it was nothin' but a disciplining, though it, like all things, came at a cost. I won't lie, it hurt me like hell, but I learned through my tribulations.

Pop always prayed that one day I'd do something great; I have to think this was all part of god's plan to bring me there, but hell, I just wish I knew where '*there*' was. I couldn't tell, just knew that when the day came, I needed to be ready, and I needed to clear my mind and soul of sin; wrath was what gripped me most tightly.

For months I could think of nothing but revenge, I just wanted to bring pain. I let go of my wrath, and it left me feelin' empty even 'til today.

I've just felt like I've been in hiding, suppressin' something fierce; I channeled it into my practice, shootin'.

Pop's pals suggested I take a place with the rangers, our local militia, I did, but I hesitated to take up my arm; 'was worried I'd go down a dark road, but these are dark times. I sometimes wondered if god would stand for what we've made of the world, if he'd still turn the other cheek to communists and tyrants, to parasites like we have today.

Times change, people say; it really scares me, how much I need to face the reality of the screwed up minds in the world today. I sometimes wish things were simpler, where I didn't need to fear violating god's word to protect it.

I needed to clear my head of these troubles, or at least take myself away from them, got me too fired up otherwise. I was still thirsty.

Outside, you didn't need to look far to see homes need repair, roads need repair, infrastructure isn't quite what it used to be. 'Was that if you couldn't maintain your vehicle, you best be able to tolerate a long walk to get to the nearest tavern, and if you can keep your truck running, you best be able to afford the gasoline, or there ain't no point to havin' it.

Pop left good connections, and they helped keep me in fuel, in exchange I keep them in reliable repair, trucks and guns, I fix it all, it's how I get by, lucky too, as 'nearest taverns 'round about eight miles out. Tavern's where you'd go for your drinks, alcoholic and non. Those with distilleries were able to keep a nice supply of the purified stuff, anything else and you'd risk sickness or worse, poisoning. The Feds still aren't too keen on our independence, but we get new neighbors every year, soon there won't be much of the old Fed left.

"Hey Del! How's the biggest man in all'a Texas doin'?" My bud James Stark called out as I drove into the Tavern parking lot.

"Ah shoot, to hell with that. All the Del Kirk legacy belongs to my pop, I ain't done nothing special." I told him getting outta my car to pat him on the back. "How've you been, bud? Your mother well?"

"She's been alright, what about you?" We walked and talked into the bar.

"Gentlemen! Del, Stark, here for a gallon or a keg?" Asked the bartender.

"Maybe a bit of both, bub. Maybe a bit of both." I took a seat, he brought us two whiskeys and a gallon of water. I'd reached for my wallet, but the bartender just stopped me.

"Don't worry, Del, you're good with us." He walked to change the channel on the bar TV. I thanked him, he smiled and gave me a nod.

"I tell ya, all a' Texas loves ya. Your pops was a damn legend, and that makes you a legend. Every damn sonva'bitch in the state knows your face." James repeated.

"'Can imagine that also stirs a man up a lot of trouble." I told him.

"Yeah well it comes with the territory, you get more you gotta defend more."

"Speakin' of defending more, Jim-" I nudged his shoulder with mine, and subtly nodded toward a feller I felt seemed out of place: He wore slacks, very clean slacks, and even though he had on a pair of workboots, he had hardly a trace of dirt on them, like he might've tried to blend in. "See something a little odd?"

"You worried? I got your back in a fight, you know that." Jim told me.

"No, I'm not worried about a fight-" I swished around my glass of whiskey, fearin' a poisoning. Jim watched me, hitting the back of my head.

"I know these people, they sure as hell wouldn't put a damn thing in your drink. You don't want it? I'll swig it here." He grabbed my whiskey, and downed half of it. "Clean." James said.

"Hell, man, I believe ya." We both turned over to the news.

"Oh, it's the uh- New England guy on the TV, uh- Doctor." James pointed out.

"Yeah, you know anything about him?"

"I heard he used to be a Nazi, wasn't he?"

"Man, shut up."

"No, seriously, like with that Commander guy and shit."

"No kidding?"

"No kidding."

"Well shit, man, that ain't good."

"I hear he's good now, I mean 'says right there he served three tours in 'Nam, and he's gotta be doing something right for New England to be following him now like they are."

"Yeah man, but that's weird, don't you think?" I told him.

"Fuck yeah, I think it's fucking weird, but you gotta go off action, not just assume things. If you just believed the stories what the news says 'bout you, then you're probably a lot worse than this guy."

"That is true. What's he done then?"

"I've got one of his pamphlets at home actually, he wants to keep people segregated because of evolution, or something."

"Huh."

"Yeah, but he's pro-gun, likes the founders, likes the constitution, doesn't like the feds, commies, or liberals."

"Doesn't sound that bad."

"No man, I think it's the damn liberals what make him look like a Nazi, they do it to everyone."

"But this guy was actually a Nazi, wasn't he?"

"Oh, yeah, but again man, I go off of action. Like you can tell me you're a good person, but if you wanna take my guns, we're not square, you know? Everyone thinks they're the hero of something."

"Right."

"This guy, I actually like what I know about him. 'Was thinking of actually reaching out to his branch down here."

"He's got a branch, like a political branch out here?"

"Yeah, wants to reunite the states that left into how the founders wanted so America can stay strong."

"That's not a terrible idea. You sure he's on the ball?"

"Yeah, I think so, man. We can check it out if you want."

"Hell yeah, let's check it out. Give the feds hell." I took another drink of whiskey when I noticed the odd fella was talking to someone at the table next to him, he looked at me, then his buddy looked at me. I kept eyeing them, one've them started reaching for his gun, so before he could, I shot him dead. His buddy drew and shot, but missed us, hit our gallon instead. "Sonva'bitch!" I shot again, and he fell hard. "Goddamn! Stark, you alright?"

"Yeah I'm fine-" He said patting himself down. "-Why the hell'd you shoot 'em, man?"

"One've 'em was drawin' his gun!" I walked over, everybody in the bar watched with only a touch of shock, this wasn't too uncommon nowadays. "Just as I thought-" I said as I dug through their coats, and pulled out a badge. "-Feds!"

"That fuckin' tears it, I can't even come to the damn Tavern without worryin' 'bout someone breathin' down my neck! We're not letting this stand no more, Del!" Jim shouted out.

"No we ain't! I've been a patient man, I've wanted nothing but for things to be right and square, but there's no use playing nice with these apostates. It's time we hit 'em where it hurts-" That's when our attention was caught by the News again.

"-Which is why the State of New England has officially declared war upon the Union. The President is gone, it is time for this zombie regime to go with him. I wish no more conflict for our fellow free states, but for all of you watching, all of you willing to finally slay the beast which destroyed our homes, come lend me your arms, come all of you proud Amerikans. Let our ranks swell so we can finally free our home. Down with the tyrants! Death to the parasites!"

Chapter 4
New York, Southern Manhattan
August 5 1975

|Garrath King|

This war of Doctors has taken a brutal character. Our march through the northern counties of New York was met with general support and at first it seemed we were welcomed saviors, though upon our arrival to the lower counties, the city that is, we were set upon by hatred and fury. Local authorities were seemingly divided in their support of us, and we found of them a tribe battling against itself.

Police, Politicians, and Counterculturals who stood united against us aligned themselves with domestic gangs and crime syndicates which opposed the order and civility we brought.
They saw only an oppressive, monstrous force that sought to destroy their ways of life, I doubt if even they realized Doctor's men perceived them no differently.

The way I saw it, the weak city-dwellers ought not hold the reigns of power; these pampered, white-collar office slaves knew nothing of the menial labor and sacrifices necessary to keep the nation functioning. It was like something out of revolutionary France, of a disconnected intellectual aristocracy, yet unlike the aristocrats, these fools owned nothing, built nothing, and knew nothing. I understand aristocracy, the few noble and intelligent leading the uneducated many laborers of a society, yet this was a seeming worst possible amalgamation of both roles. I was under an impression the rural Americans were unintelligent, yet even among the lesser of them were men who understood realities of life the city-dwellers could not fathom. The rural-types were strong men who through chance or choice of abstaining from the mainstream college-education escaped a mental poisoning that has seemingly run rampant throughout the institution.

We were treated like invading barbarians, to them, Doctor wasn't their brother, their fellow countryman, he was only an ideologically evil force of another kind than their own. It was sickening, how the sense of nationhood, the sense of belonging, had been destroyed among these people.

We devastated entire city blocks, leveling buildings to rubble, and setting fire to enemy encampments and houses. We were merciless, but only because we knew they would do no less to us, and they would. I bore witness to horrendous atrocities committed by the enemy, most commonly by their gangs, gangs of Africans who left me with nothing but antipathy in my mind and heart.

I knew well the depravity and savagery of their kind, the exploitative nature of foreign races, and their lack of respect for a culture to which they know well they don't belong to, yet of all things, I found myself halted in my violence by none other than Doctor; he'd prevented me from executing our black captives, individuals we had captured unarmed, yet certainly with familial connections to the gangs assaulting us. He saw to reminding me that they were but civilians, and to be released post-war.

I asserted that they held relations to the gangs, either directly or via a family member, that if we released them, they would only return in force to seek retribution, yet still he asserted non-criminals be left unharmed, life and liberty and all that noise. I begrudgingly obliged, but reminded him of what he told me;

"*Every threat we fail to neutralize today is opportunity for countless more to arise tomorrow.*"

I had great respect for Doctor, but sometimes I had a difficult time understanding the man, especially this pity for the minorities, minorities who clearly fail to integrate cleanly into his home culture. He justifies himself under a belief in *self-sovereignty*, that they too have a home here, though separate it must be. I say be rid of them wholly, free yourself of that obligation. It leaves me concerned of our resources, what the cost we're investing for *their* sake is, I hope it minimal. The thought of my men dying for *them*, or even some *pikey*

Irishman leaves a sour taste in my mouth. No disrespect to the big man, but serious threats are going unmanaged because of his mercy.

One does not need to take up a weapon or hold a criminal background to prove a credible threat, for example, I captured a den of what seemed to be sympathizers to the enemy, they were burning a number of maps and documents when I discovered them, but they immediately surrendered. Doctor excused this lot because they were young. We can't make exceptions; the young eventually grow up. We won't stick around to fight these mistakes, we have our own problems to deal with at home, and this cause is running its course; if he makes it unfavorable to continue, my men won't stand for it.

New York, Fort Hamilton
July 4 1976
|Del Kirk|

"The lord has promised good to me, his word my hope secures. He will my shield and portion be as long as life endures. When this flesh and heart shall fail, and mortal life shall cease, I shall possess within the veil a life of joy and peace. The Earth shall soon dissolve like snow, the sun forbear to shine; But god who called me here below shall be forever mine."

I concluded chanting *Amazing Grace* proudly to myself and my men as we prepared to deploy.

The battle of New York City was immense and ferocious, a stagnant stalemate on the field as the commander's army routed itself into eastern Pennsylvania and New Jersey.

Men just like myself from New Dixie and Deseret had lent their arms to this cause with the full support of their respective governments. Lots of my pop's pals ended up in the new Texas government, and backed me in my goal of finishing the Feds. This was the big chance to make my pop proud, 'put the last nail in the coffin of the Fed, and keep Texas free for good.

Pop's pals thought a lot of me, hell everyone did, I'm the son of Del Kirk, a war hero, I've got a lot to live up to, and I ain't aiming to let anyone down; as long as I remember god is by my side, I will not allow myself to fall.

James gave me a nod, readying his gun. I nodded back, and drew my pistols.

"Never forget; Parasites are nothing but flesh and bone!"
I declared to a roaring cheer.

We charged out, storming the fort that would gain us access to Staten Island.

"James, take demo-squad and scout-squad to the right wall! Knock it down, and survey the scene. Follow detonation with suppressive fire down the middle!" I called into my radio.

"Yes sir, Mr.Kirk!"

"Snipers, give me cover! Full-Autos stay close! We're going in." I ordered as we breached the back wall.

The entire perimeter of the coast-defending fort had been reinforced with barbed fencing and barricades. Breaching this fort would grant us full control of south Brooklyn, and air dominance for later campaigns.

I directed my men to put down any target we came across with extreme prejudice, our goal was to simply capture the fort, no survivors.

We were up against perhaps three hundred men, we were roughly fifty; fifty men mounting an offensive against a fort. As poor as those odds may seem, there's a reason we were sent in; my men, the Rangers, are some of the finest shots now on the entire coast; we've been war-hardened by the revolution, and hold no fear in our hearts for we know we are on a righteous mission against the heathens who've stolen this land.

I've been preparing for this since I was a child, and I will not hesitate to take the action that need be taken. Never again.

When I first arrived before the good Commander, I brought to him a fire and rage he held little hesitation in restricting; in conflict, anger is at times one of the most attractive characteristics of a soldier. My men feared as much as they respected me. I carried with me a precision only years of dedicated instruction could achieve, and I unleashed it like the fury of hellfire.

I indulged my sin until it grew bloated and fat. I was but a murderer, I had only yet to realize it. Soon the satisfaction of retribution weighing ten men felt little better than that of one man. I grew numb to the pleasure of revenge. I would look in the mirror, and see not the righteous avenger my father raised me to be, but a bloodied sadist; I could tolerate myself no longer. The very sight of my own face sickened me, to know I had allowed myself to fall so far into dark temptation.

It was in my hour of deepest turmoil that the good Commander approached me, I had been raving to the walls, and making a commotion in my quarters to the point it was necessary for him to confront me. He asked,

"What is wrong, my son?"

My father had raised me to defend, to avenge righteously, to obey the principles of god and our founders, but his murder, and the repeated assaults on my home corrupted my path, left me with the sole desire of destruction. The Commander told me that destruction was a necessary part of nature, *the old and weak must fall to the rising of the new and strong*; it is okay for man to destroy, but only if he does so for the sake of building something new. Harm not for the sake of vengeance, for the petty sake of *harming*, instead, simply do what is necessary to achieve a noble goal.

The Commander left me alone with those thoughts. I sat alone in my ransacked room, thinking of my father's cause, the liberation of Texas, what it all meant. I don't believe it was ever about *Texas* to him, it was about *America*, about our faith and freedom, something he so passionately wanted to protect, those were values I needed to stand for. If I truly wanted to avenge my father, it would not be through a body-count, it would be through standing by those same virtues, and destroying those who would wish to destroy them. My eyes were open.

Never again did I raise a weapon in anger. Never again would I allow myself to be overcome with a sinful desire. My actions must be for a noble purpose. I would become destruction with purpose, the flood which cleanses the Earth of evil.

I take righteous aim, and strike down man after man with deathly precision, as if my hands were instruments of correction, and as if it was through sheer will that I brought down these parasites. Blast after fiery blast shook my hands with an almost divine intensity.

I thought not of the men they were, I thought of that which they would take, those that would suffer at their hands, and in a world where they might defeat us, the cost of showing mercy to the parasite for whom mercy is an exclusive gift to its own kind.

We stood by principle, the same principle our founders fought for; to live free of an oppressive regime which was destructive to the rights of its people. Are these men tyrants? No, they are but pawns of the tyrant, in truth these are our brothers, our misguided, corrupted brothers, lost souls.

Only through death is there redemption for them; only by stopping them from inflicting the destructive cycle upon a new generation can good be achieved, a truth they do not know, and cannot understand.

New Jersey, Atlantic City
July 4 1977
|Garrath King|

A much needed leisure stay following the victory in New York, that's what this was, a well deserved reward.

We'd captured the major centers of the five boroughs, all that was left was occupation and clean up of remnants, but they didn't need us for that job, we've got more important business to attend to down toward the capitol, though not just yet, today was a day for peace.

Atlantic City, a lovely little rest-stop on our push southward. I had my *Martin* shipped over so I could drive it down the coast, showed it off to the Americans who'd probably never seen one in their lives. I was happy to see it was still the head-turner I remembered.

"Mighty fine vehicle you've got there, looks like somethin' James Bond'd drive." I was told by another captain.

"Thank you, it's one of my few treasures in the world." I answered him.

"Does it got any gadgets?"

"Gadgets?" I laughed. "It's not a real spy car!"

"I mean, it could be." He challenged. "Do you work on cars?"

"Can't say I have, not much of a culture for it as you have here."

"Well shoot, how's 'bout I teach ya? 'Name's Del, by the way; Del Kirk."

"Garrath King, pleased to meet you."

"Pleasure's all mine, I love tinkering with machines; it'd be a right privilege to work on somethin' like this." Del peered underneath the car.

"Where did you learn to '*tinker*' as you put it?" I asked in a moment of skepticism.

"My pops taught me. You should've seen the way he armoured up his truck, whooo! The thing was a damn beauty! And he'd done that all on his own on a budget! I'm sure that with military-grade tech I could make this thing a monster." He said patting the car with a look of excitement.

"I actually bought one just like this for my father, as a matter of fact. We'd hit a hard financial spot that cost us the family car, and I promised him one day I'd get it all back, I did so and then some. I'm happy to know he and mum are doing well overseas, I write to them when I can. Do you reach out to your family?"

"My uh-" He broke eye contact, and looked down to the side solemnly. "Yeah, I suppose I do each time I pray. My pops passed away during the revolution in Texas, he was shot by a Mexican prisoner. My ma passed away just one month later from heartbreak. I've been on my own ever since."

"My condolences, Del."

"It's in the past, all we can do is learn from it and focus on what's here and what's to come, right?"

"Right."

"Besides, really feels like everyone here's my family now, we gotta watch each other's backs, you know?"

"Yes, I suppose so." I smiled.

"Well then, let's get crackin' on this car! I need a good project to clear my head."

Massachusetts, Boston
June 1 1979
|Percy Holiday|

There was us three, was me, Holden, and Tyler at the wheel, driving down an empty freeway of Boston's less populated districts.

Tyler'd picked up a sweet red corvette last year, was about a decade old and could hardly start, but we fixed it up together. Before that we had a van, we took the thing on road trips all over New England, it was good for a long trip; you could recline the couch in the back to sleep, and 'had a small fridge for food; it was cozy, comfortable really, but this car was nice too; 'made me feel fast, like we were always on some kind of mission.

We'd just come back from a trip up in Maine. It was dark out now, but Boston's lights made us feel nocturnal; this was the time to be up and about.
I quickly became a night person when we finally started driving. I lived for the silent, desolate nights illuminated by nothing but the moon, our headlights, and the lights of distant buildings; 'cool wind speeding through my hair, making me feel like I was really free, like a wolf with his pack.

"Holiday, you wanna drive by the girls college?" Tyler called back. "Who knows, maybe them chicks dig younger guys like you."

Holden smacked the back of his head.

"Come on, he's too young to be doin' all that!"

"I've been with girls before." I argued.

"You been with one, Holiday! One, okay? And we buttered her up for you. That's all the experience a kid like you needs." Holden snapped back.

"Oh come on, how many chicks you done the last two years alone, Hold, huh?" Tyler mocked. "You just wanna keep all 'em for yourself, yeah?" He laughed.

"Oh shut up. Perc, you wanna pick up a girl? Because if you wanna, we've got you like... that." Holden snapped his fingers. I laughed.

"Nah man, I like a long term kinda thing."

"Bah, you're boring." Tyler mocked.

"Told ya." Holden punched Tylers shoulder.

"Yeah yeah, you get him in a girls only dorm, and he won't be singin' the same song 'is all I'm sayin'. I might just go, I wanna get me some tail tonight." Tyler pulled into another lane.

"I'm too tired for that, man. I need a coffee or something if that's what we're gonna be doin'." Holden said.

"Hold up, maybe not-" Tyler slowed the car. "You two up for an after hours movie?"

"A what?" Holden looked Tyler's direction, and spotted a movie theatre that closed for the night. "Oh damn, that might be something."

"I been eyeing this theatre for a week, has a fire ladder that leads right to the roof, meaning there's gotta be a way in through there."

"Any cameras?" Holden asked.

"None I been able to see driving by. Hell, seems like they're everywhere these days, but not many around the place. 'Think it's worth looking at."

"Shit, I'm game. Percy, you in?"

"Yeah, why not."

We took the next exit, and parked the car out of sight a few blocks down. Holden and I walked together, Tyler ran separately to lower the fire ladder. The two of us looked around for cameras casually, making like we were just walking, talking, 'looking around in case we were being watched. The coast was clear, streets were pretty vacant, so it sorta shocked us when the quiet of the night was broken by the heavy clang of a metal ladder hitting the ground with force.

"It's all good!" Tyler yelled hushly.

Holden and I climbed up to meet Tyler on the roof.
We had a beautiful view of the city from here, though we'd been higher up before, climbing one of the under construction buildings a few years back; still, we never got a vantage point of the city like this; it kinda felt like a reward all its own, but Tyler reminded us that we had a theatre to explore.

We had a door, but no handle, it was one of those one-sided deals.

Tyler dug through his wallet, and pulled out a shim, sliding it alongside the door, wedging it loose.

"Abracadabra." Tyler said pulling the door out.

"You been doing this damn too many times to start carryin' one of those with you, man." Holden said punching Tyler in the shoulder.

"This ain't nothing, 'should see the kit I have at home."

"I don't need to, man, I know you got a spiders touch with thieving."

"Less talk, more walk." Tyler said leading us in.

The door led us down a flight of stairs, passing one door that was locked. Holden and I walked down to the lobby.

"You two go ahead, I wanna see what's behind this door." Tyler called.

"You got it." I fired back, hopping the lobby counter, and lifting a pack of candy.

"Don't rot your teeth there, Perc. 'Heard of a kid in a candy store? I feel that's you right now."

"Yeah yeah, I'll be alright."

"Toss me a box, will ya." I grabbed a box and threw it to Holden who wandered off toward the theatre rooms.

"Hey hold up!" I scooped up some leftover popcorn in one hand and ran to catch up. "There's nothing goin' on here-" That very same moment the screen lit up, and I could hear the projector whirring.

"Hey fellas!" Tyler called out from above us. "Check it cool!" Some ads started playing on the screen. "Think I figured this thing out-" The sound boomed so loud I was sure it could be heard a block away.

"Damn it, man! Turn that shit down!" Holden yelled covering his ears.

The sound eased up, and some movie started playing; 'something about a guy who builds himself a girlfriend. It's probably the tenth film about robots to come out this year, and it wasn't even a good one, but I wasn't here for the movie so I didn't give a damn.

Holden took a seat, chomping on handfuls of his candy. I relaxed a bit after the scare that booming music gave me. I leaned up against a chair, and picked at my popcorn piece by piece.

After a minute I told Holden I was gonna keep looking around, he said *'alright'*.

There wasn't much to the lobby, but I liked the atmosphere, something about the neon lining being the only light in the whole place; the sound of the movie playing in the distance. I just hopped back behind the counter, and poured myself a drink from the fountain, hung out there to take in the moment. I grew calm, and the minutes whizzed by, my head had gone somewhere, but I was brought back to reality by an approaching flashing light of red and blue.

"Oh sh-sh-sh-it." I bolted over the counter and into the theatre room. "We gotta bail! Cops! Cops!"

"Cops!?" Tyler yelled, peering out from the projector room.

"What'd I say?! Yes, cops!" Almost immediately Tyler dashed out, knocking over the projector.

Holden and I ran into the lobby where an officer was shining his light in through the glass doors with what must've been the manager of the place unlocking the door.

"Go. Go, go go go!" Holden hushly yelled, pushing me toward the stairs.

"Hey! You two, stop right there!"

We weren't willing to wait around. We downed those stairs like they were collapsing. Heavy footsteps followed behind us, I knocked open the roof door. There was no sign of Tyler, but immediately I heard the cocking of a gun, and I froze.

"Stop right there, make no sudden moves." Yelled an officer. I complied.

Holden, who was still hidden behind the door, was pinned by the officer coming up the stairs.

The officers cuffed us, and told us we were under arrest. Before they walked us back down the stairs, I could see Tyler's car driving off a block away. He'd ditched us. Holden said it was better one of us get away than none of us, but I could tell he was upset about this too.

We'd spend the next six hours in the cold precinct holding cell. Holden was exhausted, but not given to falling asleep on the dirty jail floor. It was maybe nine or ten the next morning when an officer came in to finally speak to us.

"Alright boys, you have good news and bad news. Bad news is the theatre owner is determined to press charges for damages to an expensive projector, on top of breaking and entering, so you could see some real jail time, maybe as much as ten years; it's such a shame, young boys like yourselves, you've got your entire lives to live-" This choked me up a little. "-But there's good news, very good news. You're both of conscription age, healthy enough I'd assume to be breaking and entering." He pulled out two forms, and handed them to us. "New England's looking to forgive some young first timers in exchange for military service. You'd be working in the reconstruction, possibly serve as occupancy in a nice town or city in the west, see a little combat maybe. Two years, each of you, then you're free."

I looked at the document titled "New Amerika" for a moment, then looked over at Holden; he was smiling optimistically.

Washington D.C, Jefferson Memorial
June 2 1979
|Mister Doctor|

Our forces had crept well into Federal territory; Neu York had become a central node from which we could begin spreading into the industrial sector of Pennsylvania and the Great Lakes, while routing an invasion of the governing district here in Washington.
I had with me a division comprised of South New York, Metro, and Jersey brigades, supplemented by Dixie's personal liberation corps in the South placed directly under our own command, leaving me a totality of some eighty-thousand soldiers to topple the Federal army on their home-field.

"Colonel-Captain Bull, what's the status report from recon team?" I called in as I plotted our movements. Jefferson's statue stood stoically behind me, instilling in me a sense of inspiration, reminding me that this too was a war for the liberation and redemption of our founders from the slanderous tongues of hateful Marxist revisionists poisoning all they represent.

Raindrops clinked off the metal barricades which reinforced the monument to protect it and our base of operations from enemy fire. Though secured by the bodies of water which surrounded it, we still kept artillery, two tanks, four hundred personnel, and a dozen helicopters at the ready in the event of an enemy air or artillery strike.

We had D.C closed off on the South and Eastern sides, hopefully that will soon be true for the North as well, but we were not dependent on that outcome; our goal had been to take the White House from the South and declare official victory in the war.

I was to meet with General Jackson of Dixie for the next phase of operations in the East, he and President Davis had been at the forefront of Dixieland secession, and the two felt more than obliged to support us in this ultimate defeat of our common enemy. Jackson was a good man, Davis too, his cousin Colonel-Captain Rob Cobb Davis had personally lent to us a volunteer army of some five-thousand men whom we've integrated as Rebel Brigade, and distributed as needed into several companies.

"Manpower is fair-" Bull responded over his radio. "-They have some fifty-thousand personnel supported by an iron wall of tanks and helicopters down the National Mall line. More concerning is rumors about those automated turrets were true, we're looking at some couple hundred scattered between the Washington Monument and the White House alone. Helicopters have a good grasp over low-concentration areas, and may push onto base-camp, but our artillery should smoke them down before they approach a threatening range. The tanks and turrets are what I'd be most weary of; as I said, we're facing an iron wall that needs to come down before we can even consider an advance." Bull radioed back.

"What's the status of your front?"

"Stable, sir. The usual business."

"Surveil the scene for a control or power grid of sorts, that may provide us a solution to the turrets. Otherwise, continue sniping and reconnaissance operations as you were. Radio your demolition team to coordinate a series of tank strikes along twelfth avenue, that might just allow us to cut their Eastern forces from the rest, and move in for a kill." I responded.

"Sir, that'd be suicide; regardless, my demolition men are too firmly preoccupied with-" I cut Bull off to contact Fuse.

"Colonel-Captain Fuse, I need an expendable demolition team in the East. I believe we can move in reinforcements to crush Federal forces there if we cut them off from the central Mall."

"Yes sir. Would you prefer I send in one of Dixie's Negro squads?" Fuse answered.

"Send in whoever you feel appropriate."

"Affirmative, sir." I tuned my frequency out to contact Dirk.

"Colonel-Captain Dirk, any updates on a solution to the barricades?"

"Yes sir, Commander. I've constructed with our engineers two prototype weapons which ought give you plenty of options; firstly we've built off an old schematic that'd never been put into military use, we're calling it the *Red-Glare*, and it is in essence a rocket-launcher for miniaturized nuclear warheads; advantages include a wide damage radius, with a yield of some twenty tons, and residual radiation which ought be fatal to anyone unlucky enough to survive the blast."

"Not a fan. Ideally we want to minimize damage to monuments and the environment, can't rightly reconstruct a fallout-zone, at least not for a while, and we're looking at a relatively cramped battlefield, I don't want to risk exposing our own men to that material." I signalled one of my officers to ready a helicopter while I continued conversing with Dirk.

"Alrighty, sir. Alternatively, we've devised something with more surgical precision-" Our conversation was cut-off by a heavy bombardment which rocked the ground beneath me.

"Commander Doctor!" I heard an officer yell out. "We're under attack from across the basin!"

"Raise the artillery, and return fire!" I shouted back, preparing myself to evacuate to a new base of operations when suddenly I was knocked hard to the ground, and deafened by a blastwave that left me coated and surrounded by a cloud of debris. The bodies of several officers laid broken to my left and right. Only I and two others survived the impact. I looked up to the statue of Jefferson, it had been ravaged by the blast, but still stood proudly, like a Roman ruin; it had protected us from the blast.

As I looked around myself to the devastated monument, I felt a burning anguish boil in the pit of my stomach, rising into my chest, and sending a shock through my spine into every part of my being. My hearing began to return as I heard someone call out,

"Commander, the evacuation team is ready!" I rose from the ground, helping my officers up before calling into my radio once more.

"Fuse-?"

"Yes, Commander." I heard him clearly.

"Bring me five hundred tanks, and five hundred helicopters. I'll be personally overseeing the rest of this operation myself."

"Y-Yes, Commander." He understood the severity of my order.

"Dirk." I called in.

"Yes sir, Commander."

"How quickly can you produce and supply our front with those weapons you mentioned to me? I want thirty units. Not a single one more."

"Give me a few hours, sir." As I switched frequencies, my surviving officers and I mounted the helicopter to regroup with our men in the East.

"Bull?"

"Yes, sir?"

"Tell your men to get off their asses or I won't hesitate to wipe them off them map along with the Feds."

"Yes-" He strained. "-sir."

Chapter 5
New York, Kingston Training Facility
June 4 1979
|Percy Holiday|

We disembarked the transport bus, and were immediately met with the regimentation this place was to instill within us; a man with his hair tied behind him in a short braid greeted us sternly.

"Listen up, recruits! My name is Colonel-Captain Fuse, you will only address me as Captain for the remainder of your term at this camp! This is one of our largest camps, with two more of equal size in the New York region alone. Here we have five companies of two hundred men each, for a total of one thousand men at capacity. I lead Yankee Company, of which, most of you will be joining. Those of you who do not make the cut for any reason will be transferred to Bulldog Company under Captain Bull. You do not, let me emphasize this, ***NOT*** want to be an American, especially an ***Irish*** American in Bulldog company! You ***will*** die there, I am not mincing words with you. Seeing as you've all come out of the Boston penal system, I assume most of you are of Irish ancestry, so take precaution, obey my orders, cause no trouble, show no weakness, and your stay here will be both positive and productive. Understood?"

Some of us nodded and hushly agreed.

"I said is that understood!?"

We all shouted "Yes, Captain!"

From that moment on it was nothing but instruction.

"Three more miles, maggots!"

Every morning would start with a five mile run.

"Steady hands! Fire!"

Every noon would be practice firing. For every centimeter you missed the bullseye per shot, you could expect ten pushups.

"What do we do when the mag is empty!?"

"Fix a bayonet, sir!"

Practice firing would be immediately followed by a bayonet charge.

"Protect your face, maggot!"

Afterwards was close combat training with Yankee Company vets, each of them easily twice our weight in muscle. 'Soon felt as though I wore a near permanent shiner.

"This is the part of the day I look forward to most-" Holden said scooping a ladleful of gelatin cubes onto his plate. "-Dinner."

Dinner was the best meal of the day, a reward for good behavior, as it were. Breakfast would sustain you, but was a bare-minimum meal: Biscuit. Apple Sauce. Ham Steak. Water. Every morning with no variation, dinner on the other hand was a varying assortment that ranged from breaded chicken to salisbury steak.

"'Helluva lot better than prison food, 'ey Perc?" Holden nudged me, I nodded, a little hesitant to agree solely because of how exhausted my body was.

"Tired, huh?" He asked.

"Yeah man, I'm not sure I can keep doing this." Holden laughed at my comment.

"Well what are you gonna do? Go back to jail? Hell-" He hushed his voice. "-Don't think these guys'll even let you. Might just shoot you dead for desertion or something." I looked around, the worry on my face was clear to Holden. "Look-" He said. "-I get it hurts getting into this routine, man, but this right here, this is our life now, you don't just give up on life because things are hard, you gotta push through. Pain's only temporary, man, you're gonna kick pain's ass, and we're gonna be livin' free just months from now! We'll never have to do this again after that, man! Imagine you and me sippin' sodas on a hot summer beach, pickin' up chicks." That image took me away for a minute. My worries subsided. "Hell, and nobody'll be able to call you little after this, think about it, we're gonna be goddamn beasts leavin' here."

"Yeah, maybe you're right."

"Maybe I'm always right! All we got is two years of this, then we're free. That's not even how long school is, man! Two years and then we're free!"

Holden's words got to me, I didn't really realize it just then, but it gave me something clear to aim for, and that made for enough of a push to keep me going with a smile.
Every morning after that, I'd start my run with the proud thought that each day I did this was one less day that I would need to repeat it; one day closer to freedom.

That thing I wanted more than anything, to get out of here, it made me reach further, and kept my engine burning brighter and longer, but something else made me slow down just a little. It occurred to me one day during practice firing, it occurred to me that I was really training for combat, that I could die.

"What if I don't live to make it out of here?"
I thought out loud.

"Holiday!"
Captain Fuse had yelled. I shot up immediately, and stood straight.

"Yes, captain! I know I missed, I was just about to-." I yelled back when he cut me off.

"Shut up, Holiday! You've demonstrated remarkable improvement, enough to warrant the attention of Captain Dirk, head of Ranger company."

"I don't understand, sir. Am I being transferred?"

"Temporarily." He responded. "-but you will be returning to Yankee company come deployment. Captain Dirk happens to be one of the finest shots in the entire army, and happened to take a shine to you, as in he would like to teach you to be a better shot so that you can bring some of those skills to Yankee company, to be quite frank, I greatly appreciate it. Follow me, I'll introduce you to your new Captain."

We drove out to the deep end of the camp. We'd only ever go out here to pick up weapons from the armory.

Ranger company was famous for their deadly accuracy, resilience, and weapons crafting, nearly every one of our gunsmiths were a member of Ranger company.
Word was that the original fifty members who founded Ranger company all came from out west to support the Commander's Revolution, 'so skilled that not a single one of the original fifty has died in combat, at least that's how the rumor goes.

We'd disembarked, and I was guided into Captain Dirk's office before Captain Fuse abruptly dismissed himself. Dirk was facing away, polishing a rugged revolver when the door was slammed behind me.

"Percy Holiday." Hearing my own name shocked me stiff and into a salute as Dirk set his revolver up on a shelf mount.
"You're the young man I'll be instructing?"

"Y-Yes Sir."

Dirk laughed casually at my nerves. "You're not in court, Percy. Ease yourself. Take a seat for now."

I looked around, seeing a fancy couch and some just as expensive-looking chairs.
He had a very nicely kept office; it had a southern elegance to it, with a touch of safari hunter.

"Those're some awful nice guns." I said, looking at his wall of mounted weapons.

"Oh, well thank ya, most of these are my own fabrications. I specialize in anti-material guns. Being a mechanic and gunsmith, I figured out that there're some good exploits to stop a vehicle, be it a car or a tank. 'Way I like to see it is that I build armor as tough as I can, then I try to build a gun strong enough to break that armor, then again try to built an armor to survive that gun, it's a good work cycle, I imagine you must have one as well, given that when you first got here you were lagging far behind, now you're pushing far ahead, heh, what gives?"

"I set a goal, sir-" He cut me off.

"Just call me Dirk, bud. No need to toss '*sirs*' and '*captains*' around my way. My name's Del Kirk, but you can call me Dirk, most all folks do these days, helps differentiate between me and my pop, 'don't rightly like strangers calling me *Junior* now." I remained silent. He cracked his knuckles, sensing I had a hard time being casual with officials. "So tell me 'bout this goal of yours, what's moving you?"

"Well, Dirk, I actually just want to get this all over with, and go home to my life as it was."

"'That so? And how's that philosophy apply to you risking your skin on the field? 'You gonna be a soldier, or are you just gonna, as you put it, '*get this all over with*'?

"Well-"

"Better question-" He cut me off again. "-are you afraid of dying?"

"Yes."

"Why?"

"No one wants to die."

"That's true, but we all do, and we never know when it might happen. Why, I could shoot you as you leave my office, and you'd never even realize."

"Are you going to shoot me?" I said with a slight panic.

"No, bud, but someone might. You may get shot on your way home, your bus might crash and kill you before you reach your home; you might be killed in your sleep the day you get home by an intruder. We all die, and rarely do we see it coming, this is truth, but you don't let these thoughts haunt you day to day, do you? You've only just awoken to how vulnerable life is because suddenly death has occupied your mind, but you must push it out and accept that this is your life now, it does come with risks, but we take those risks so there's something worth coming home to. Without pain, without sacrifice, we would have nothing.
Percy, you came here with a friend, right? Holden?" Dirk picked a file up off his table, rereading it. "What're you gonna do when your friend is out there in the field and he dies to protect you? What if everyone here is killed, and you're all that's left? Will you be happy that you survived? Or will you wish you could have done something? That you could avenge this loss, better yet, stop it from happening?"

"What are you saying, Dirk?"

"I'm saying, in this world you are all that stands between life and death, you can save what you love only if you're willing to take that bullet for it. We live free at the expense of many before us. You must have something you value deeply; what is it that you want to go home to? What's that something that gets you out of your crummy little cot every morning, out of your rundown little house, to take on what life might throw at you because it makes it all worth it? Ask yourself if life is worth living without it."

"With all do respect, sir, that's pretty talk and all, but it don't do much to make me feel better-"

"You're not answering my question, Percy; what do you want to go home to?"

I struggled to put my vision into concise words: *My friends, adventure, good times*, I tried to say it without sounding so petty, to figure out what strung it all together.

"Think about it." Dirk said as he walked away, picking up the mounted revolver he had been polishing.

"This was my father's revolver, Percy; fear was the difference between his life and death. I was young, and green as a leaf-" He chuckled, trying to hide how much he hated speaking this outloud. "-I uh-" He choked up. "-I had to kill a man, Holiday. I'd been trained to, I knew how to, but I was scared. I didn't pull the trigger, and he ended up pulling one on my pop. It was just one second after that when I finally got the courage to do what had to be done, the moment I realized my fear cost me the most important person in my life. You, Holiday, not us, not the army, ***you*** are the only one you can count on to protect that which you hold dear, and you must ensure you are willing to do what is necessary when you're put to the ultimate test. The price of peace is constant vigilance, but you can't even seem to see the danger on the horizon. We need to sharpen your vigilance. If you love something, Holiday, you best hope you learn to protect it 'fore it's gone. When your world is ripped from you, there's nowhere to hide anymore; you finally face the fear, but it's too late." He grasped my forearm.

"No more running, you hear?" He gripped my arm, his face intensified into a serious glare as he demanded I answer the question he'd asked. "What do you love?"

I thought of only the time I'd spent with my friends, the brotherhood we shared, continuing it once I got out of here, and how I feared losing all these adventures I promised myself if I were to die in combat, I began to realize how selfish it seemed.

"What are you fighting for!?" Dirk shouted in my face.

New York, Kingston Training Facility
July 3 1979
|Percy Holiday|

Under Dirk, I continued my training routine as I had previously, with the exception of moments in between my activities to reflect on why I am training: a ten minute period of giving thanks for what I have, reminiscing over what has passed, and striving for what's to come.

Dirk encouraged me to pray, even if I wasn't religious, to project my desires for myself to the world, or nature, or some higher power, and ritualistically offer something in return for the gift I requested. For strength I'd submit to carry a heavy load during my run. For courage I'd part with a personal comfort of mine. For clarity I'd purge my system of distracting excess. He taught me to be a child to the god of nature, that nothing, no skill, trait, or thought will simply be granted to me, I must give something up to receive something in return. If I work harder, I will be rewarded. I must trade my sweat, my time, and my ounces of will for the gifts of health, wealth, and wisdom.

Dirk told me it's easy to take for granted god's gifts once you've received them, but it's not a one time transaction, it is a committed relationship which in the end enriches me as a man.
I am given strength so I may labor more, and I labor more so I may gain more strength.

"Once it becomes easier-" As Dirk put it. "-God isn't telling you to rest, he's helping you to do more."

Work did become easier, I could run further and faster with less effort, but I felt wrong to slack behind or half-ass it just because I could.

I had laid a standard out for myself, and I was determined to hold myself to it. Dirk would know, nature would know, it was in my control to do right or wrong.

You can't lie your way out of a fitness test, or a test of survival, and this is what I realized in all my sittings, that life was all about at its core: fitness and survival, if you're not fit, you don't survive, and if you don't survive, there is no life to live.

New York, Kingston Training Facility
July 4 1979
|Percy Holiday|

I awoke to an unusual morning call, instead of the typical wake-up bugle I was gently roused awake by the sound of a fine violin playing over the loudspeakers, I recognized it as *Ode to Joy*, and it occured to me that today was Independence day.

Training was called off for all five companies: Rebel, Saint, Bulldog, Yankee, and Ranger, all of whom were out and about the training grounds; it was the most active I'd ever seen the place.

"Hey Perc!" I heard Holden calling out. Me seeing him outside of dinner for the first time in almost a month.

"Finally a day off, huh?" I laughed, shoving him.

"Damn straight." He stretched his arms. "I'm telling you, man; these days are going by like hours. We're gonna be out soon. I can already taste those cold sodas." Part of my mind felt grim, remembering that we were still only in training, and the worst was yet to come, but I quickly reminded myself of what Dirk taught me, that this isn't just about serving my time, it's about doing my part to make sure there's something for me and Holden to go home to, and not only for us, but for everyone who looks forward to sodas by the beach or to late-night blockbusters with popcorn bags the size of watermelons, being able to look forward to barbeques and road trips, hell yeah I was looking forward to doing it all again, but it started to mean all the more to me that maybe my grandkids or just other kids who grew up like me could experience it all too.

"'Ey Perc, you alright? Think I lost you there for a minute."

"Heh, yeah, I-I was just thinkin' about it, man. I can't wait."

"You know I'll make it happen, if I need to drag your ass out of fire, you know I'll make it happen. Anyway, as much of a day off as it might be, I still have a list of things to do from the higher ups, what's on your to-do list, man?"

I honestly didn't have much to do, cleaning the barracks would be a snap since they're usually always kept neat. Holden was happy to hear I had a clear schedule because he was determined to get a taste of our old shenanigans, even if it was only for a day.

"I've been hearin' 'round the camp about a pretty sweet vehicle in one of the hangars; a suited-up, armored sports car, never been driven since it was put here; whoever owns it never takes it out, but today-" He twirled a ring of keys around his finger. "-that changes." A wide smirk filled up his face.

"Gosh, Holden-" I scratched my head. "-this sounds too risky, it don't sound like something you'd go for unless you were sure we'd be good."

"And sure I am, I've eyed the hangar it's supposed to be in, and not once, not a single time have I seen anything but a military truck drive out." He pointed out to the far distance at a particular hangar in a line of eight.

"Alright, say hypothetically it is in there, how you suppose we're gonna drive it out?"

"Get this; We take a truck, one of the big supply carriers, load the car onto the trailer, and boom, it's ours for the hour. Trucks are going in and out of town anyway to pick up supplies for the festivities, no one'll be the wiser."

"Eh, alright, but say it doesn't fit?"

"If not, then that's the end of it. Worst case scenario, it's not there; best case, we get a joyride for the day. What do you say? You wanna take this ride with me?"

"Aw hell, yeah I'll do it, why the hell not."

"That's the spirit!"

I had a receding feeling that we'd regret this, but I was eventually completely overcome with a premature sense of freedom, something which almost made me even more uneasy when it would occur to me in moments of greater clarity that we were likely stealing a higher officer's car.

Before I knew it, we had ran the length of the training field, reached the hangar, and made our way inside; it was right there, just like Holden said.

"Holy hell, she's a beaute." I let out.

We were looking at a car out of a *Bond* movie. The thing was sleek and gleamed from every angle, yet was plated in a clearly strong metal.

"Look at that-" Holden said knocking on the thick car door. "There's really no way to even sledgehammer that door in. Thousand bucks says it's bulletproof." Holden hopped inside of it.

"Thousand says it's bombproof, even." I offered back.

"Leather seats, man." He said admiring the interior. "This thing is a king's car."

"Okay, let's load it onto the truck, we don't want someone to walk in on us now."

"A'right, I'll open the trailer, you take the wheel, and drive it in." Holden said while on the floor of the car.

"Wait, how am I s'pposed to start it without the key?"

"Hot wired!" Holden yelled out, giving me a thumbs up as the engine came to life. "I'm gonna start the truck, you hop on in!" Holden climbed out, running up to the truck. My dreadful thoughts were back in my head.

Part of me wished we wouldn't have found it, but I didn't want to back-out when I told Holden I was in.

I opened the left door, but saw no steering-wheel on the drivers side, it was on the right. Suddenly it struck me.

"Holden!"

"Yeah?" He called back.

"This is a British car!"

"So?"

"Who would have a British car!?"

"What're you-?" He looked out the truck window. "Oh sh-!" Before he could finish, I was violently yanked from the car, and brought to face an intimidating giant of a man.

"Pikey." He growled in a heavy accent, spitting in my face before slamming me onto the floor. "You best get out of here too, you little mick, 'less you want a piece 'a me!" He yelled at Holden, then knelt over to look me in the face. “I don’t think you know who you’re fuckin’ with, yah little bastard. What’s my name?”

“I-I don’t know!” I coughed with panic as my breath returned to me.

“There’s a sticker on the car ‘says *Johnny Bull*. I’m fuckin’ Bull, who the fuck are you?”

Holden rushed to my side, trying to guard me from any attack Bull might have considered inflicting upon me.

“We’re very sorry, sir, we didn’t realize this car belong to you! I take full responsibility for this, I shouldn’t have brought Percy into this.” Holden said, shielding me.

“‘So yer the brains of the operation-” He dealt a heavy shot to Holdens gut. “-piss off then, your penalty is knowing your friend here will suffer for your mistake.”

“No-!” Holden resisted, taking an immediate kick to the hand he was clutching his stomach with.

“My judgment is final.” Bull said grasping my forearm, only to be once again interrupted by Holden, putting himself between me and our attacker.

“So is mine.” Holden uttered between coughs.

“We have no room for thieves in our ranks, you pikeys are no different.”

“We’re-” Holden coughed heavily. “-We’re sorry, sir. I made my mistake, I won’t make it again.”

Bull looked Holden right in the eye, he grumbled and released me.

"I respect your loyalty to your friend, you've got some sense of moral. I'm going to trust you only made a mistake, and leave you as is, but do not tread where you don't belong." Bull growled.

"Yes sir." Holden agreed, the two of us helping each other up and out of that place, Bull eyeing us as we left. I realized as we reached the exit, how quietly such a large man would have had to move to sneak up on me like he did. I assumed Dirk might know a thing about this fella, but he'd told me not to disturb him until it was time for the festivities,
July fourth was an important day for Dirk, and he preferred to spend most of it alone to reflect, but I still wanted to ask one of the higher-ups about Bull, so I went to Captain Fuse who was not surprised to find Holden and I had been clobbered by the fella.

"Bull's a complex guy." Fuse told me. "His story's too long to tell. He's been with the Commander almost as far back as I have. Frankly he's started acting like he really doesn't want to be here, meaning he's a lot meaner than he used to be. What you gotta know is that he's been refining his skills for years; he ain't the leader of Bulldog Company for nothing. The guy's basically a silent assassin, big as he is, he's got the footsteps of a spider, and that's not even mentioning how ferocious the guy is just plain head on; most people he's dealt with, like he did you, don't live to tell the tale."

That was inspiring to me, to have been face to face with someone so skilled in combat, I was eager to find out if he'd teach me anything like Dirk had.

I went to the Bulldog company barracks to speak with him directly, but he seemed less than happy to see me.

"Now what'd I say about treading where you don't belong, pikey."

"I wanted to officially apologize for myself, sir. I understand that this is a military institution, and I'm not here to play, I'm here to learn to be a better soldier. My actions were out of line, and I will not be repeating them."

"Lovely, anything else?" He asked dismissively.

"I came here to mend ties between us because I do not want to cut off the skills I think I could learn from you, sir." He shifted in his seat, grinning, though skeptical of what I'd just said, so I clarified. "I believe you can teach me to be a superior soldier, sir. If you'll accept me, I'd be humbled to learn under you." He couldn't help but burst into laughter for just a moment.

"Am I suddenly a wise old karate master? What makes you think I'd want to take time out of my schedule to personally train the likes of you?"

"I'm not part of your company, but you are indisputably one of the most skilled men at this camp."

"Clearly." He uttered.

"I can't imagine any immediate reason for you to want to train me, but know that I am determined to do the very best I can for our cause, and I believe that the better my teacher, the better that I can be."

Bull furrowed his brow and scratched his chin.

"I don't think so, pikey. Piss off now."

A bit of an embarrassing moment for myself, I mean, really I expected little different, but it was worth a try, still I was not disheartened, and still I was determined to learn what I could from Bull, even if he wouldn't teach me directly. I wanted to know what he knew.

It was beginning to get on in the evening. Word was that the Commander was coming in to give a speech before the firework show.

I introduced Dirk to Holden that evening as we set up the last bits of the event for the night. Holden was still apologizing for getting me mixed up in that situation with Bull, but I'd told him it wasn't bothering me none. Dirk had commented on our encounter, and told me that when Bull was a kid, he used to climb buildings just like we did, 'was a "*thief of some kind*" Dirk told me, the irony of that brought a laugh out of me.
Fuse, who had been setting up along with us commented himself, saying that Bull likely just had it out for us because we were Irish, that and the fact we touched his precious car.

"Aw hell, you were messing with the man's car?" Dirk asked.

"It was stupid, but yeah." Holden said. "What's he got against Irish anyway? He's British, isn't he? Ain't they pretty much the same?"

"Apparently not." Dirk answered.

"No no no, you've got a major misconception-" Fuse started. "See, Bull's English, British is just anyone from those islands, and England specifically is in the south, the people who live there are typically Anglo-Saxon Anglican Protestants, right? Irish on the other hand are nothing like that, they didn't even speak English until pretty recently. See, the Irish are Celtic and Catholic, big distinction, and the two don't like each other because the English basically colonized the north of the Irish island. Now the Anglo-Saxons are Germanic basically, they have their origins in that region of Europe, the Celts however, they likely came somewhere out of Anatolia or Greece, and migrated up, historic record might even suggest the origin being in Thrace because the people here were notable for their light green eyes and red hair."

“What?” Holden said with a face full of confusion. “I’m sorry, did you guys catch any of that?”

“Yeah, I get it. It's like the English and Irish are just plain different cultures and people entirely.” Dirk answered.

“Right.” Fuse said.

“How do you know so much about this?” I asked Fuse.

“I mean this is basically my bread and butter, I used to trace family lineages, and the history of human migration for Doctor’s old party, or rather the party before Doctor’s party.” Fuse answered.

“How’s that work?” I asked.

“Well, like, names for example; Del, you know your family history, like, where your family’s from?” Fuse asked.

“My family’s from Texas.” Dirk answered to be met with a laugh from the three of us.

“Right, but your last name’s Kirk, that’s a Scottish last name, but you don’t really look too Scottish. I see probably a lot of English, and maybe a little native, which would make sense because a lot of Scots moved to the South, and a lot of English moved to Texas.”

“Hey, cool.” Dirk smiled at Fuses analysis.

“And Percy, your last name’s Holiday, that’s got roots all over Britain, which could make you English, Scottish, or Irish, but clearly your features are purely Irish, your family probably just came here one or two generations ago, am I right?”

“Yeah, that’s right.” I laughed.

"The name's also common among some Negros because during the first big Irish migration, the two were basically in the same class, so it wasn't uncommon for an Irishman to take a Negro wife here in the states, I believe we've got a Negro in Yankee company with just a variation of your name, *Hollydade* I think." Fuse added. "Personally I think the Negros should just get their own company, but there's probably just not enough to justify one, so they sorta spread them out between us and Rebel company, surprisingly they've got a lot of Negros on their side, but that's just because they've got a lot, period."

"New Dixie is doing the same segregation policy Doctor is, ain't they?" Dirk asked Fuse.

"Yeah, but they're actually moving them to new all-Negro communities, one in the North-West and one in the South-West, kinda like India did with it's Muslims by making the two Pakistans in it's East and West. Doctor's just keeping borders how they are, but creating no-crossing zones for White and Negro communities, and you know, that's great, I say let them do as they want in their own homes, and vice versa. It ain't right for to force together two people who can't get along."

"Yeah, I guess that makes sense." Dirk said.

"Damn right it makes sense; if it were up to me I'd send them all to one spot, and wall if off. I get it, they've got good people among them, and right now we're fighting for the same cause, but we're two totally different groups with ultimately different ideals and cultures. Sure, I think they're still Amerikan, and we've got an overlapping history, that brings us closer in cooperation, but they're not us, and they can never be us, vice versa. I think you all well understand that living in a Black Amerika wouldn't be the same as living in the White Amerika we all know. Can you give me that much, Del? Does that *jive* with your lib philosophy?" Fuse mocked.

“Look, I get it.” Dirk said. “I just don’t like to discriminate personally, but I understand the reality of where we are.” Fuse dismissed the argument, knowing he could go on.

“Anyway, Holden, I didn’t get to you, your last name’s Collinfield, right?” Fuse prepared to analyze Holden.

“Collinfeld, actually.” Holden replied.

“W-w-wait, ‘***feld***?” Fuse inspected Holdens name tag. “This says ‘***field***!”

“I know, it’s a misprint.” Holden answered confusedly.

“***Feld*** is a jewish suffix, are you a jew, Holden?” Fuses friendly demeanor disappeared.

“No, I-I mean I don’t think I am, my parents are Catholic and my grandparents came from Ireland.” Holden answered worriedly as he realized Fuse was interrogating him, and had placed his hand on his sidearm.

“Is anyone in your family jewish?”

“No, nobody that I know!”

“Have you ever celebrated a jewish holiday or have any openly jewish friends?”

“No, my neighborhood’s nothing but Irish and Italians!” Fuse seemed to calm down after Holden’s answers.

“Well, you don’t look jewish anyway. I’m gonna give you the benefit of the doubt, but if you so much as give me a reason to believe I can’t trust you, I’ll have you expelled from here, and dropped right into prison.” Fuse said mere inches from Holden's face.

"Why does it matter if he's jewish?" I asked in honest curiosity, Fuse looked at me as if the answer was obvious, turning to Holden and asking him one more question.

"Collinfeld, what are you, and what country is your home?"

"I'm Irish-American, America is my home."

"Scratch the Irish, Collinfeld, is Ireland your home? Do you believe in the Catholic Church more than America?"

"No sir, this is the only home I know. I gotta believe in America first."

"That's right, if your loyalty isn't to America first, you don't belong here." Fuse stated. "Now, Holiday, the problem I have with jews is that loyalty is almost never for the country they live in, because before being a citizen of that country, they are, above all else in identity, jewish, and their loyalty is to the jewish people, not to America, not England, not Ireland, to no country but to the international jewish nation. For most peoples, when you take away their country, they die out, but when the jews lost their land to the Romans, they spread out, and survived; held together initially by their religion over thousands of miles, and later through a shared identity as an eternal foreigner to every land, and when you have no loyalty or sense of duty to a land, you exploit it, you survive off of it's body while it withers because you can always just move to a new one. Do you know what that is? A parasite."

We all remained silent. Finally, Fuse broke the silence in an apology to Holden.

"I'm sorry for my accusation, Holden, even if you were a jew by blood, which you do not seem to be, you've as of far been a fine recruit, and for that, are deserving of a certain level of trust. I apologize."

Fuse dismissed himself, and left us with our thoughts.

Come sundown, the camp was abuzz with stringed lights, music, and laughter; I'd almost forgotten this was the camp I'd been training at all month.

"The Commander will be delivering his address shortly. Gather around the stage before it gets too crowded, and as always, ***May Freedom Reign****."* A voice announced over the loudspeaker.

The area facing the platform was quickly becoming packed as the entire camp gathered for the Commander. He arrived with a motorcade of armored trucks, stepping out to greet his audience. He strode onto the stage in a navy blue suit, and red slacks with a thin white pin-striping, he'd been dressed as Uncle Sam.

As he approached the podium, it took only a moment for the crowd to quiet. He grinned and spoke into the microphone,
"Happy Fourth of July."

The crowd cheered in response.

"Five years ago New England said in one voice that it would refuse the infringements of our liberties imposed upon us by the subverted old American Regime. Nine years ago, even before us, the Free State Of Texas declared its independence from the Union; I mention this in recognition of Ranger company's recent return from the occupation in the south, and for having stood with us throughout our campaigns; they are some of the finest soldiers a nation could ask for." The audience applauded.
"Five years ago we, not as New England alone, but as a New Amerikan Order, made up of freedom-loving Amerikan men, came together in a declaration of war against the socialistic, hedonistic order which had hijacked our nation. Today-" He paused in a smile, looking throughout the crowd as a group of men in the back cheered. "Those men back there are excited for good reason." There was a

brief laugh among us. "Today I am very proud to announce that the Old Order has collapsed! Washington D.C is now ours!" A roar of joy erupted from us all, I only recently being made aware of the state of things.

"Now, there's a great deal of unorganized territory which has come under our domain, from the states of Ohio to Oregon. There are few remaining insurgencies in these lands, but they do exist, I have thus authorized state governments to assume temporary autonomy until these regions can be properly organized with the cooperated oversight of our auxiliary corps. Understand that my intention is to fully reunite our nation, preserving state local autonomy, while maintaining the united strength we hold that no other nation knows. We, across this extensive land, live widely varying lives, one set of laws is unfit to govern so diverse a people! But different as we may be, we are one family, the Amerikan family, and we protect each other. You may live a Dixie life or be a holy-man of Deseret, but Amerikan are we over all else, an ethnically white nation-state built by pioneers, inventors, and freedom fighters upon the virtues of bravery, ingenuity, and liberty. Within us alone lies Amerika's future, no other people but us could create such a nation. An example has been left for us by our founders through their own labor, their own diligence, their own dedication; men who were not merely handed Amerika like a gift as we were, but who had to forge it themselves! It is up to us and only us to preserve and ever improve upon the model our founders built, to do otherwise would be to spit upon the face of your deceased father as you torch the home he built for you to grow up in!" There was power and passion in every word he spoke. "The Old Regime was an awakening for many of us, a realization that we'd become mad as a nation, a schizophrenic state driving in opposite directions. We were asleep to the fact that we as a nation were leading a double life, edging our body ever closer to Communism, if not for the awakening jolt of the radical, brazen policies the Old Regime imposed upon us, we very well could have remained unaware for decades, by which point the damage could have been too extensive to mend." There was a brief pause of solemn reflection on that fact. "Thankfully, that wasn't the case. New York is now a safe state freed of the liberal, communistic scum which for so many years made it a den of corruption and sleaze. New Jersey is seeing steady occupation and development into an outside base of operations for the cleansing of Denver and Maryland where a number of loose insurgencies remain. We are witnessing the beginnings of a great rebirth! As the America of our founders was to the Roman Republic, so is ours to that of the Empire!" A chorus of pride swelled. "There of course remains one last stronghold for the enemy, and that is the state of Pennsylvania, where citizens caught within zones of enemy occupation endure brutal conditions and oppression at the hands of rogue military personnel. It is because of the heavy enemy concentration within the region that we will take extensive occupational action in the territory. We are counting on you all to take back our land when we deploy with the rest of the South New York Brigade in the upcoming weeks. Will you take it back!?" He boomed.

We all chanted '*Take It Back!*' with the vision of our new goal firmly illustrated in our minds, and with that vision we pledged our determination to reconquer the state, and free our people.

With the speech concluded, so did the night sky shine with the launching of the fireworks. The booms and cracks of glimmering red, white, and blue, the cheers and chants of a zealous crowd, it all came together in an explosive energy of pride, confidence, and power.

Later that night I was tasked with clean-up duty like the rest of the boys; they put me to work near the stage. Most were respectful enough to take their trash with them, but things always fall, and someone's got to clean it up.

The noise died down to crickets and distant chatter. The lights still glowed bright like they would in a carnival. The scent of sugary fried-dough and other celebratory treats still spiced the air, making the menial task all the more enjoyable, just to spend a little more time in this extremely pleasant atmosphere.

"Excuse me, recruit." I heard a man call out behind me.

"Yes sir-? Commander!" I said, startled to find the Commander standing behind me. "How can I help you, sir?" I saluted him as I felt I should.

"At ease, Mr.Holiday."

"H-How did you know my name?"

"Your name-tag." He gestured to his own as he replied. "I hope I'm not taking you away from important work." He half-joked.

"No, sir. I'm just about finished."

"Be assured that you can return to your cleaning once were done. Walk with me."

"Yes, sir. Am I in some sort of trouble, sir?" I said suddenly reminded of our trouble with Bull earlier.

"No, nothing of the sort. How'd you enjoy the speech?" He asked as we walked through the alleys of festive tents.

"Inspiring, sir. It feels good to be reminded what we're pushing toward, and what we're fighting for, we're not just here for kicks, we all want something, and this is how we're gonna build it."

"And what is it *you're* fighting for, son?"

"Honestly, sir, there was a long time when I wasn't sure, I'm a little ashamed to say it may seem a bit selfish, but all I wanted was the security of knowing that my friends and I could live freely to experience all life had to offer, but recently I've been thinking hard about my own life, my mortality to be accurate; the risk of dying terrified me, it meant I wouldn't get to experience all those things I wanted to do, and I guess part of me secretly felt like maybe I could live forever."

"But you can't." He answered with a dull smirk.

"But I can't. I don't even have the right to live to be a hundred-"

"That's a luxury and a gift only time and nature can surprise us with." He added.

"I don't even have the end of a day promised to me. All I have are these moments I'm experiencing right now, it's a story that ends, and I don't know when."

"But you can decide how the story goes, if you're creative enough."

"And so what good was my old goal? We all want to feel good, feel and see exciting things, but what good does that leave behind? I mean, I take all that with me when I'm gone, the only thing that feels worthwhile, that I feel will last after I'm gone, is if I do something good for others, really, I want to make sure every kid knows what it's like to have real friends, and live moments like mine, not live just ***for*** them, but get to live through them on their way to their goal. I was real alone growing up, I had trouble with other kids since kindergarten, and it wasn't until I met my buddies that I really started to feel like I belonged somewhere."

"We're all one big family here in Amerika, it almost seems like we've forgotten that fact in recent years, that we just let anyone join the family until it wasn't one at all anymore, I grew up through that, you did too, and I pity your hardship. I was dealt a hard hand since birth, my upbringing was anything but tolerable. From so young an age I felt something was deeply wrong with our home, our country, I wanted nothing but to fix it. I came to wish I could bear the burdens of my fellow countryman for them, I felt the sole purpose of my life was meant to be sacrificed for the salvation of my people, but there was so much more to it than that; nature and hardship gifted me with a set of skills which made me an adept soldier and mentor, I was cast a role to play in the story of my people, one which may well cost me my life, but that didn't matter, what mattered was that I put my skills into practice, I could not merely ignore my divinely ordained path, and I believe neither will you." He smiled as we came full-circle in our walk around the camp, back in front of the stage where we had begun. "I'll leave you back to your work, son. I have a feeling you'll make me proud."

Chapter 6
Pennsylvania, Philadelphia
December 20 1979
|Percy Holiday|

We stomped through inches of snow in heavy black boots, carrying rifles which in the hands of ordinary men would hold a hefty weight, but to us felt as natural as our own arms.

The order and synchronicity of our marching formation was only contrasted by the combat we'd see; our regimentation would take on a form of controlled chaos, scattering in all directions, only to systematically and surgically eliminate rogue military and guerrilla soldiers.

We were merciless in our actions, taught that every potential threat we left standing would create countless more to face soon after. No liability could be taken.

Blocks of soulless apartment complexes would be razed, pieces of degenerate art set ablaze, the monuments of our founders would be protected, secured by our wills and lives.

We felt as though we were engaging in a cleansing act; the world came to look so polluted by filth, lies, and decadence, like waking up to a landfill in your own backyard; the only solution was a swift and extreme one.

Traitors, just as our founders believed, deserved a traitors death; capture would assuredly get you hung; surrender would earn you the bullet.

There was no room for weakness or compromise, from either them or us. So extreme must we act so our sons need not face the horrors we endure for them, and so do we endure these horrors so our homeland is secure.

A perfect world would see no wars like this, of men pitted against their own misguided brothers led so astray by subversives, liars, and manipulators; so too might *they* see us this way, no different as we see them: misguided and ignorant, but our world has basis, a history, and an identity; theirs is but a counter-identity, it's only purpose being to exist in violent, hateful opposition to our own; it is a parasitic ideology, both in its practice, and in that it cannot exist without a host identity to poison, corrupt, and deceive.

Months of rigorous training had made us all into hardened warriors.

Under Dirk I'd become a deadly shot, renown for my pistol work to the point that my sidearm quickly became my preferred weapon, and I'd carry an excess of ammunition on my person to suit my style.

From observing Bull's training regiment, I learned quickly how to scale brick surfaces, and move with stealthy silence, making me the prime candidate for a number of recon missions.

"Holiday! Take out that machine gunner!" Captain Fuse yelled out to me from his cover behind a truck.

Bullets were flying from every which direction. I ran from cover to cover until I reached an alley sided by two brick buildings.

I grasped tightly to the slightest ledge of each brick, and pulled myself up to the top where I leapt from rooftop to rooftop, coming under fire from men positioned up in these vantage areas, though unprepared for my speedy assault.

I had placed myself in position behind the machine gunner. Having a clear line of sight from the roof, I took up my rifle and aimed, but as I shot, I was knocked from the roof, only managing to grab my assailant at the last moment, sending him falling with me.

I caught myself on a third floor window, attempting to climb my way back up to take the shot, when suddenly I heard the machine gun platform creaking, I turned my head to find it rotating my direction.

Panicking, I drew my pistol, barely holding on with one arm, firing upon the machine gunner, but he'd been well protected by a metal plate; there was little that mere handgun calibers could do to penetrate it.

Upon hearing my gun click empty I was filled with dread, I could've died there if it wasn't for Fuse and Holden who ran a charge toward the gunner as he turned toward me, executing him, but also exposing themselves to surrounding enemies.

In a moment the two were set upon by a barrage of bullets, only ducking for cover behind a car in the knick of time.

"Holiday, we need coverfire!" Fuse yelled.

I pulled myself to the roof as quickly as I could, evaluating the scene; things looked bleak: they'd cut us off from our men some hundred yards back, Fuse and Holden were surrounded on all sides by at least twenty hostiles, and I was without a weapon.
I'd lost my rifle in the fall, so I picked up one of the enemy's guns, I hadn't any training with it, but it was the best I had.

I took aim, and shot down three men on the left side.

"Left's clear! Watch your back!" I called to my friends, offering some protective fire as they moved for better cover, but as they moved opposite me, I became unable to target the source of fire that was coming from under my position, someone inside the building was firing from a window and had them pinned.

Looking over the edge, I could see the gunfire coming from the third floor, so I rammed in the roof-access door, making my way down, and reloading my handgun before I breached the apartment.

I heard the gunfire stop as the door came down. I moved silently, but found myself tackled by a heavyset, armored man with a knife, he'd knocked my gun from my hand, and made two sharp thrusts with his knife into my torso; I felt an icy shock through my body, and I instantly retaliated with a weighty punch from my metal plated gauntlet, knocking him off of me, giving me just enough time to hide.

He lumbered back up, scanning his surroundings for me.

Quickly spotting my gun, I leapt for it, instinctively pointing it straight at my attacker, and unloading the magazine into his body, sending him collapsing back into the wall.

I took only a moment to catch my breath as my friends were still under fire.

I made it to the window when suddenly my body felt weak, I was bleeding out, and Holden could see me struggling to stand. Despite the clear risk, Holden dashed out from the safety of his cover, rifle in arms, to come to my aid.
Knowing I was in danger was enough for Holden to say "*to hell with it*" and do what needed to be done, we looked out for each other, nothing got between that.

Like a berserker, he sped through a hail of gunfire, returning it to sender. For a moment, I thought I saw him recoil as if he'd been hit, but it didn't stop him.

Captain Fuse looked aggravated, but couldn't leave Holden to fight alone, and followed close behind, covering him as best he could.

"Percy! Percy, are you in here, man!" I heard Holden yelling through the stairs.

"I'm over here!" I called out, leading him to me.

"Shit, you're losing a lot of blood."

"No shit-" I coughed.

"Watch the damn language, Perc! Lay down, we've got ya." He dug through his backpack for some sprayon stitches. "This'll stop the bleeding. We're gonna get you out of here, Perc." He helped me up, carrying some of my weight so I could walk more easily.

"It's not good, men." Captain Fuse told us as he walked in. "I think we came pretty damn far, but they've got us cornered in here. I laid a trap on the stairs, but after that's gone off, there's nothing standing between us and fifteen, maybe twenty more guys-" An explosion went off in the building, and Fuse reloaded his gun. "My last magazine. Holden?"

"I have two left, sir."

"Holiday?"

"I'm not going down without a fight, sir." I pulled my second handgun from my holster, holding both up.

"Good man. It's been an honor serving with both of you. I'll buy you a little time. Prepare yourselves." Those were the last words we ever heard from Fuse before he walked out to exchange bullets with those sons of bitches.

"You ready, Perc?" Holden asked.

"Yeah, just lean me up against the wall, then take some cover."

We got into position.

The moment we spotted them, we saw to unleashing every ounce of lead we had against those parasites, holding them off, but soon realizing the scope of our situation; I was almost out of ammo, Holden was out entirely, and they kept coming.

Holden tried to fight them off, only getting himself shot.

He fell next to me, I handed him one of my pistols as they swarmed us, but almost out of nowhere they started to retreat, running out of the room to bolt down the stairs.

Suddenly the attack stopped.

We heard heavy steps come up the stairs. We braced ourselves, but then there walked in the Commander, clad in a heavy plated suit, bringing a rescue party close behind him.

Pennsylvania, New Philly Base Camp
December 24 1979
|Percy Holiday|

I'd been released from the medical office just earlier today, but I ended up coming right back to pay Holden a visit.

"Hey, man, how're you holding up?"

"I tell ya, I ain't got the slightest clue how you're up and about while I'm still bedridden for the next week." He said clumping up a magazine page, and throwing it at me.

"I heal up fast, man. They had to pull some lead outta you. Me, I just got some stitches." I told him, patting my sewn-up wound.

"You lucky sonvabitch." He threw another crumpled magazine ball at me, laughing. "Well, nothing's left to do now but catch up on some readin'. Check it out." He flipped the catalogue over so I could see the cover. "Cali's got phones you can put in your pocket now, ain't that fockin' wild? Hey, how's Op-New Philly going, by the way? I'm hoping we at least did all that for something, you know?"

"Word is we've taken the whole Eastern half, still defusing Harrisburg, and pushing through Altoona, but otherwise we've secured half of the state."

"We're making real good time, they said it might take a few months to get the whole state under occupation. Any word about who's going to take Captain Fuse's place in leading Yankee company?"

"Right now the Commander's taken charge of the company, but he's aiming to merge Ranger company and Yankee Company under Dirk as a single battalion for the occupation." Just then, we heard a pair of familiar heavy boots stepping through the halls and then into our room.
"C-Commander Doctor." I stuttered and saluted immediately, Holden doing the same.

"At ease, gentlemen. I've come to personally congratulate you two for your sacrifice and show of courage in the face of danger." He held up two small boxes, and presented one to each of us. "These are your purple crosses, wear them proudly."

"Sir, thank you, sir." I said.

"Lieutenant Holiday, Major Dirk and the late Captain Fuse have spoken to me at great length about you."

"Good things, I hope, sir."

"That's correct, I've actually been looking for a young man much like yourself for a time. If it's not an inconvenience, may we speak somewhere privately?"

"No inconvenience at all, sir."

I excused myself from Holden's room, and followed the Commander back to his office.

"Holiday, I've brought you here because you've been nominated for a promotion."

"A promotion? Well, thank you, sir."

"Don't thank me, you've had a good teacher, Del, Dirk rather, is the finest shooter I've ever met, and I met some very good shots during my time in 'Nam."

"You served in Vietnam, sir?"

"Yes I did, I was probably just a little younger than you are right now when I first enlisted. Remind me, what brought you into the military, son?"

"Honestly, sir, it was my only alternative to prison. I had gotten into some trouble with the law."

"I see. How do you feel about the military now?" He said as if it was the answer he was expecting.

"I'm happy life brought me to it, this has given me a lot of purpose." I said, bringing a smile to his face.

"It does that. I say it isn't until you've been given the challenges of survival that you really evaluate what's most important in life." He paused. "I've noticed in addition to your shooting, you're also an adept climber, fairly tactical too, some of the newcomers have even started calling you *Doc Holiday*."

"Yes, sir, I'm aware I've developed something of a reputation around the camp. I take my training very seriously, but I believe that if I do only the training everyone else does, well, then I'm only as good as everyone else."

"And where did you learn to become so tactical?" The Commander asked, very likely knowing the answer already.

"I attempted to replicate Captain Bull's training regiment so I could do what he did without needing him to teach me."

"Did you ask him to train you?"

"Yes sir."

"And he refused?"

"Yes sir."

"I assumed so. That was very resourceful of you, Holiday."

"Thank you, sir."

There was a minute of silence, as if he were evaluating the conversation.

"Holiday, you're a highly skilled soldier with a natural drive for self improvement. You have, in your time here, risen to the top of Yankee company, and demonstrated great resolve in combat. You are an excellent example for the new recruits."

"Thank you, sir."

"That's not all, I have a position lined up for you to train newcomers following the end of this operation. If you choose to accept it, you'll be able to put your tour here toward our *New Order G.I Bill*, you'll be given a forty thousand dollar starter on a home, son, that and an additional hundred dollars a week until you're settled into a job."

"I don't know what to say, sir."

"Just say you accept the position; if you can churn out more men like yourself, it'll be more than worth our trouble, hell, it'd be no trouble at all. We treat our soldiers right, especially the best among them."

"Is there a chance I'd be able to make *this* my job, sir? It seems strange to say, but part of me feels as though I've been searching for precisely this for a lot of my life. I like the brotherhood, I like the tough training, I like the rewarding feeling that I'm making a change. I know there are others like me, those who feel outcast, lost, drifting through life without purpose or family, and I want to give to them what this experience has given to me. I was fortunate enough to find good friends who kept me on a fairly straight path, but that easily might have not been the case, and for others, that is their reality, so I want to be there for them. If I can make a career out of that, I'd be a very happy man."

"I can absolutely arrange for something once you're released. You have a bright future in the military, son."

Pennsylvania, Altoona
December 25 1979

|Garrath King|

Del and myself had been tasked with an important reconnaissance mission. Doctor had tracked-down enemy leadership to a single bloke who'd essentially taken control of the rogue military and left-wing factions, quite frankly I'm surprised anyone could manage; while the military was cohesive and formidable, most surrendered the day the capital was captured, save for a handful of extremists and rogue terror-cells which splintered away. The Communists, or Leftists, on the other hand were fairly sparse and disunited, which surprised me considering how much activism and pull had occurred pre-war, very puzzling, but I chalked it up to cowardice, regardless, that means there are still several threats among us, even if dormant; I encouraged Doctor to adopt a more draconian approach to weed out the traitors, if only temporary; he's employed curfews, searches, and raids until conflicts officially end; to be safe he'd best maintain them until the potential threat is reduced to negligible proportions, but to each his own.

"This entrance is sealed up tight, think ya can manage it?" Del asked, tapping on the vaulted door.

"A fools task. Give me but a moment." I informed as I took to picking the lock. "Right as rain." He cranked the valve as I defused the lock, keeping the door in an unlocked position.

"Bee-utiful. We've got a hallway past this door, right?"

"I believe so." I said as we changed places, myself now holding the door closed while Del unholstered his revolver.

"Think we've got a couple hostiles beyond this point?"

"I'd assume most certainly."

“Alrighty-then.” Del took a breath. “Breach.” On his mark I pulled the door free, and he charged in. I could hear his shots ring loudly above the brief bursts of enemy fire. Upon hearing him yell “Clear!” I moved in tactically past the office-lined hall to provide silent support in the main foyer, placing myself behind enemy-lines while Del kept them preoccupied from the front.
It didn’t take much long for us to converge upon the last man, bringing him down.

“Once again, well done, my friend.” I commended Del.

“As always I’d say we make a pretty damn sweet team.”

“Rightly.” The two of us made to surveying the area for the documentation we were looking for. “I heard you’ve been training that pik- er, Irish lad.” I brought up as conversation.

“Yeah, he’s a good kid; I get the potential the Commander sees in him.”

“Can you believe the boy asked me to train ‘im too? Ha!”

“‘Could imagine. Why’d you turn him down?”

“You daft, mate? You know I don’t like his kind. Nothin’ but trouble-makers or ass-kissers, his lot.”

“Trouble-makers? Considering your reputation, that’s not an accusation you should be throwing around, you and your company.”

“Bah, my boys are just tired of this ***Amerika*** noise, they’re really a good lot; I could give the order to die, and they’d obey without question. They’re nothing like them pikeys we’ve been busing in.”

“We’re all the same blood here, Garrath. It don’t matter to me where Percy’s parents came from, so long as he’s Amerikan.”

"It's that same talk what let's the Negros and Mexicans claim themselves no different than you. There's a line to be drawn, making it wider destroys what it means to belong to a country."

"Maybe so. I like to think that so long as you love this country, and give something to it, it's enough, but I see your point."

"We get along awfully well, I'd say. You were raised in Texas, I in Britain, but we both share English blood, and I believe on some level that we both recognize that, recognize that we're part of the same tribe, like brothers."

"Funny to put it that way, maybe we do." Del smiled. "-but I still stand by my point. We're not all English here, and we ain't Germans, or Spanish, French, or whatever the hell. You guys have that problem in Europe, that differentiation, here, we're just whites, and it's the damn same for the blacks; you think they've got any idea where exactly they came from? Hell, I didn't even know my family was English until you and Fuse started talking about my last name. I'm a White Amerikan, dammit, and so is Percy, now I'd say that's all he need be!"

"Hm." I took a moment to think on this matter. "What if he was a Texan? Would that alone suffice, or would it require him be a Christian? And the same of Deseret, for him to be a Mormon? There's more to it, isn't it?"

"Now what are you on about?"

"You suppose that America be more united than Europe in this singular White identity, but if that is so, why has it divided as it has along such clear regional identities, the Southerners in Dixie, the Mormons in Deseret for instance. Didn't Doctor himself state how diverse the cultures of this former nation have become? Mark my words, Dirk, while today you may still be united as Amerikans, given enough time, that identity will fracture further until Texans and New

Englanders are no more united than the French and us English. Know your blood, know your culture, and preserve it alone. A union such as this cannot withstand."

Del dismissed me, 'told me he had faith in Amerikan unity, though he did surrender that perhaps every time and again a *culling of the herd* would be necessary, much as this war had become; he quoted Jefferson in saying "*the tree of liberty must be replenished by the blood of tyrants and patriots*". I agreed. Nature drives us toward chaos in all things, men of order are needed to maintain the structure of the state, something I believe we English have done better than perhaps any other. I suppose it's not too far-fetched for the Amerikans to endure, after all, who says empires **must** fall?

The two of us delivered the intelligence we recovered back to base, we had a confirmation of name and location: Commander Nemo, he was held up in Fort Pitt with a sizable army behind him. I had my reservations in participating my men for this following mission. I had been very tolerant of Doctor's command out of respect for the man, but we had more than outdone ourselves in contribution to his war. Still, if this was indeed the final enemy stronghold, the prestige we'd receive upon our return home would be immense; it would assure that Doctor uphold his promise of providing us his nukes and erasing our debts. I'd been directed by home-command to secure this special relationship of co-prosperity with the Amerikans so we could proceed with our rebuilding of the empire, but this has carried on for much longer than anticipated. I'd be putting my men at tremendous risk; we have an invasion which could easily last one day or one-hundred days. I find myself incredibly conflicted.

"Garrath, we're getting an incoming message from-" Del took a moment to read the notification. "-Oh." He seemed a bit off-put. "It's for you, Garrath."

"What is it now? Bad news?" I asked, he hesitated to answer. "Let me read it, here." I walked over to give it a look. As I read word by word, my stomach sunk, my hands grew cold, and I felt weak. The message read:

"Dear Mr.King, please accept our deepest sympathy for the loss of your father, George Edward King on the evening of December 23rd 1979. Upon the personal request of the Prime Minister, we've been entrusted to relay this message to you directly as a courtesy. It has been an honor to aid you in maintaining communication with your family while you face combat abroad. For you, your father has left an inheritance of-" I tore the page, unable to read another word.

Pennsylvania, Harrisburg Base Camp
December 30 1979
|Garrath King|

"I'm standing by my men on this matter, I refuse to follow through on this mission!" I asserted to the commander over the map on his table.

"We've discussed this, Bull, you and your men are to stand by my side until the war is over." Doctor said calmly, pointing down to the map.

"The war's been won! We took the capital months ago! You said that would be the end of it!"

"Enemy leadership fled to Pittsburgh, this is their last stronghold, and we have them surrounded on all sides. Once we capture Fort Pitt, your men will be free to return to England, and our arrangement will be completed."

"This is too dangerous-" I argued. "-they have the entire city, and a concentration of men we haven't seen since the battle of New York! I am certain that if we march in there, some of my boys won't live to see England again!"

"That has never been a problem in the past, now has it? This situation isn't as grave as it seems, they have no supplies, and no allies left." He challenged, to which I explained,

"They're desperate, this is their last stand, and it will be a bloodbath! Now I've continued to bring you fresh recruits from my land because you promised me again and again that we would return an army for the English people, that you would compensate our country proper for the pain ***we've*** endured, but time after time you've prevented us from going home, ensured us that we were but one more fight away from freedom! My men have just about had enough."

"Your men are the most unruly lot in our entire army!" He shouted, standing up. "Of them I've heard nothing but complaints: Excessive force, abuse of civilians, misuse of military resources-"

"Abuse, misuse-" I mocked. "What's this about misuse, then?"

"Why don't I begin with the fifty pounds of nuclear material you allocated for that vehicle of yours?" He answered, returning to his seat calmly.

"Now hold on there, that was Del what did that; the bloody grease-monkey made my car so damn heavy that he had to build it a damn nuclear engine."

"That makes you no exception, Captain Bull. You and your men made a promise. ***I*** made a promise, a promise to send you back as soldiers; how do you expect me to return an unruly gang of men who can't even finish a job."

"What's stopping us from forcing our way out?"

"Death, Bull, if you desert us now, the penalty is death. We've discussed this before." Doctor answered me.

"We won't go down without a fight." I said.

"But eventually you will go down." He claimed, glaring at me in a moments silence. "This is the last battle, Bull, I guarantee you. Whether we win or lose, whether they escape or not, this will be the last battle your men need fight. Let us finish this as we intended." Doctor stood and extended his hand.

"After this battle, we're done." I stated.

"You have my word." He answered. I shook his hand.

Pennsylvania, Monroeville
December 31 1979
|Mister Doctor|

How fitting that it should come to this.

Pittsburgh had housed a substantial cache of gold and weapons stowed away in a bunker which the Commander and I intended to recover post-collapse; however, circumstance left me confined to the North-East. With the Commander gone, and the party shattered, there was no one left to retrieve our other caches, we were, after all, the only two who held official knowledge of their locations, that is, unless someone had stolen said intel from the Commander's records: A spy.

I had at last found him, the Commander's assassin; he was held up in Fort Pitt, leading the remnants of the opposition; he had been involved in the war since the beginning.

How sweet that he should be the last head of the socialistic serpent to be severed.

As much as I'll need restrain myself, we ought to take him alive before proceeding to execution; the more I learned of him, the more questions I had:

His name is Nemo, singular; he used the last name 'Smith' in his membership application, but we determined it to be false after the fact, leaving us with just Nemo: latin for '*nobody*', most certainly a pseudonym. Earliest records place Nemo in the United States around the mid-fifties, but he's an older man, likely in his own mid-forties, meaning he's certainly a foreigner with no upbringing in the states, though skilled enough to mask an accent, and infiltrate a party like ours with falsified documents and stories without rousing suspicion.

There is no doubt in my mind that this *Nemo* didn't just fall into these circumstances, this is the work of an active agent with a plan, one that'll finally meet it's end; though still I must know for certain why it began. To destabilize the United States, perhaps? Assure a victory for the Soviets in the Cold War by dividing us? It'd be ingenious, really; if we took no action, and allowed ourselves to succumb to socialism, they would win, and yet, having retaliated against our system as we had, we've divided ourselves into warring factions; this is why New Amerika is so crucial: unity and sovereignty, it's our only hope for sustainable freedom and security.

I hesitated at my desk as I oversaw and refined our invasion plan, my focus was caught by the glimmer of a bullet poking out of an ammunition box.

"I ought just end it." I said out loud. Half of my life has known nothing but war and death, and it's all added up to this. I wanted to know why, to have the satisfaction of understanding what drove a man to kill my country, before I killed him. It may well not at all matter, what matters is that he has done what he has done. Death is the only suitable punishment for a monster.

Now, for the battle at hand: We mobilized on Christmas morning. I was routing Bull's company through Monroeville for a direct northern and southern land push into the city through the east. Fort Pitt is fortunately located on the opposite side of the city; however, reinforcements could no doubt be deployed to our positions in a matter of minutes, so I've ordered Virginia's Eighth Rebel company to advance from Wheeling onto the Monongahela river, and rain artillery fire on the fort to keep their men occupied, and if possible, cross the river, capture the fort, and converge on the city with my men.

Bull was unhappy to find our front was completely comprised of his total reserve of men; admittedly I could have easily called in Yankee company to bolster Bull's numbers, but I believed this would be an instructive experience for him; though in the beginning he and his men were dedicated, as our numbers grew, so did they grow comfortable, lazy, over confident to the point that my word was no longer rule, only Bull's was. Try as I might, the drunken punks within them couldn't be snuffed out, my authority was not respected, my instruction went unheeded, my men sacrificed tenfold to keep them alive. It didn't matter to me how skilled they had become, only that they lacked the discipline to put these skills to admirable use. I promised an army would return to England, but many of these men were still thugs just like their captain, not from a lack of instruction, but from poor leadership, and yet they still expect me to compensate them in raw nuclear weapons. I will deliver onto his nation the proper resources I promised, but it ***will*** come at a cost, and Bull will be made to understand that.

Pennsylvania, Pittsburgh
December 31 1979
|Garrath King|

I hadn't endured such a deep sorrow since the raid on Doctors compound. We'd begun our spearhead into the city, populated by close to 100,000 armed men; at full capacity, my men numbered only nine hundred, by the fourth hour of combat, I had just under two hundred.

Our mission, as Doctor put it, was to lead the way for surrounding forces to engulf the city from all sides; we broke the enemy, they cleaned up the pieces.

We carried superior weapons, superior armor, and had the support of an armoured division, but the enemy was seemingly countless in number.

Our years of training threw sheer odds into our favor, but as time wore on, our numbers atrophied, and as many as we took, it was not possible for us to last so much as another hour in that city.

It filled my heart with a dreadful anguish each time I witnessed one of my men succumb to a stray bullet, to a misstep, or a sloppy mistake.

By the time we'd reached the fortress, I was reduced to twenty-five men, supplemented by Doctor in an armoured vehicle with only four others. Our reinforcements had begun to take the outskirts of the city, and secure the now disorganized regions, but we were still alone; no one could help us.

Pennsylvania, Fort Pitt
December 31 1979
|Mister Doctor|

We were navigating the inner halls of the fort, bombardment hitting hard the outer walls, and quaking the ground as we ran.

We broke-up Bull's remaining men into three squads; I led one down the south halls, Bull leading another through the north halls, and one sent into the courtyard; all three of us were to meet at the opposite end in hopes of locating Nemo, and eliminating as much resistance as possible.

Fighting directly alongside Bull's men showed me firsthand how well versed they had been in combat, yet unfortunately, still undisciplined; one man stealing from the pockets of those we shot, another, always pausing to comment on a kill, both of them having been shot while distracted. The surviving eight refused to take my direction, and insisted on doing things as Bull taught them.

In the moment of ceasefire, our argument over direction had escalated to a heated point; they were furious that so many of their company had been slaughtered, and of course I was to blame. They lined up to corner me, yelling back and forth how they were going to shoot me dead, but before they could, some resistance-men turned a corner, and opened fire on us.

Bull's men acted as a shield that allowed me to duck into cover, swiping a rifle off the ground, and shooting upon both, leaving me alone to converge on the end corner of the fort with Bull; he was in tears, already waiting when I arrived.

"That's it; they're all dead." Bull said. "All my men-!" He forced through painfully as the rockets crashed and exploded beyond the fort walls. "-are dead." He nodded his head, and looked directly at me, laughing miserably. "You were right-" He harshly smeared his hand along his face and chin. "-this was their last fight." His despair faded in a fit of heavy breathing, and morphed into anger. "**You knew this would happen-!**"

I also knew what he would do next, so just as with his men, I acted; I shot him. He clutched his abdomen before I shot his shoulder and leg, dropping him to his knees.

"I'm sorry, Johnny. I hoped your men would prove me wrong, but they're not fit to defend a country, not under your guidance."

"***You bastard-***" Bull grunted as I continued my search.

"Yes, let it out, Bull. I had very high hopes for you, and your men, but I want soldiers, not mercenaries, our people deserve better."

"You just wanted to get rid of us-" He mustered. **"-you used us! Used us to fight your dirty war!"**

"Heh, and we fought ***your*** dirty wars: WW1, WW2, what place does America have in Europe? None. Yet your fathers pulled mine into your little pissing contest with Germany, and what'd it get us? The Bolshevik revolution, and the rise of the Soviet Union to the level of a super power! Now I find out the commies are likely behind this whole catastrophe, so here we come full circle. Consider this recompense for the sins of your father; rightful retribution."

"You're insane-" He forced.

I left him to take his final moments in solitude. I followed a staircase to the war room, if Nemo was here, it's the last place he could be hiding.

I threw open the door at the bottom of the steps to find a bearded man with black, slicked-back hair; he wore spectacles, and a red armband like the rest of his soldiers; he was armed with a revolver which he dropped to raise his hands.

"I surrender." He stated with a grin.

"This has been a long time coming, Nemo."

"Excuse me?" He said in a sudden Brooklyn accent. I held him at gunpoint, ensuring no one else was in the room.

"Save the games for interrogation." I called into my radio to cease bombardment, and send in an evacuation team. ETA would be approximately twenty minutes, so until then, it was just me and Nemo. "Take a seat, we have some time." I gestured to a chair in the corner of the room, keeping my barrel fixed on him.

"Didn't realize little ol' me would be such a priority target." He continued in the convincing phoney accent.

"Cut the crap, you son of a bitch. I ought shoot you right now."

"I'm sure you have the wrong man, Doctor, but if it keeps me alive, I'll play your game." He said snickering. I was ready to take a knife to this smug bastard.

"Oi, mate-!" I heard call out behind me. I turned around to see Bull slumped up in the door-frame, rifle in hand. "**-Bugger off.**"

Pennsylvania, Fort Pitt
December 31 1979
|Garrath King|

"**-Bugger off.**" I said firing off a volley of lead into Doctors torso, sending him collapsing back onto the war table. "**-Fuckin' bastard.**" I was still bleeding heavily, clutching my stomach tightly with my shot arm. I collapsed myself in the door-frame, when all of a sudden that man in the corner of the room stood up and clapped.

"Very good!" He cackled in a hard eastern-european intonation. "That could have gone very poorly for me had you not shown up when you did."

"Sound." I remarked sarcastically.

"I see you are in need of medical assistance, fortunately for you, you are in the presence of a real doctor, though unfortunately for both of us, we will both be dead within minutes if we do not escape." The man yanked a tube of sprayon stitches from his shelf, and gave me a temporary solution to the bleeding.

I slung my arm over his shoulder so he could help me to walk.

He led me to the courtyard where one of our armored trucks had been left. He helped me inside before starting the ignition, and taking off.

Pennsylvania, Fort Pitt
December 31 1979
|Percy Holiday|

“Doctor! Do you copy? Evac team is here, what is your location?” We were getting no response; we had to assume the worst. “Search party, fan out! Commander’s non-responsive!” We scoured the fort, Holden and I following the trail of bodies and ammo to a stairwell that led to a wooden door, upon kicking it in, we saw the commander there on the table

“Commander!”
I ran to his side to check his vitals.
“Stay with me, sir! Please!”

I could sense a pulse. His armor was heavily damaged, but he was alive.

“Medic! We need a medic to the western edge of the fort! Down the stairwell! Hurry!” I called into my radio, bringing two medics to find us. They began treating Doctor right there.
They pried his armor off, finding that most of the bullets were caught, but three did pierce through, and struck Doctor’s upper chest. The medics checked his breathing, patched up his wounds, and rushed him to a helicopter outside. Holden and I rode back to camp with Doctor and the medics, I prayed he’d pull through.

New Jersey, Atlantic City
January 1 1980
|Augustus Doctor|

I awoke in a plush, comfortable bed; this was a comfort I hadn't known for so long. The sheets felt freshly washed, the mattress had a subtle spice of old cigarette smoke, my pillow felt cool and soft, the whole room was comfortably cool as a matter of fact. I could hear the slight whir of an air conditioning unit cooling the room.

I climbed out of bed, my feet met with the tender brush of a short carpet, though my eyes were still hazy and unfocused. I navigated my way to the restroom, feeling a familiarity with the layout of this room, a familiarity I couldn't quite place.

Upon reaching the sink, I could finally see clearly; this was a hotel room. The sink came complete with those standard, little, generic soaps and shampoos, and I looked, as best as I could put it, refreshed, as if I were no older than twenty; I was clean shaven, my hair trimmed, my face with hardly a wrinkle or scar. I was taken aback by my own reflection, yet I couldn't look away.

My attention was drawn away by the whistling of a coffee machine settled atop a mini-refrigerator; I had a complimentary pair of disposable coffee cups to serve the drink into, but no milk, just some packets of sugar. I took my coffee, sipping it black as I gazed around the room, it was small, but contained everything I ever needed out of a room: a bed, a desk, a sofa chair, two nightstands, and a small television; that was all I needed to sleep, work, relax, store, and relax some more.

The entire end wall of the room, opposite the door, was draped by a set of curtains, I wondered why. Reeling back the curtains, I saw the wall was a large sliding glass door, the glare from the sun made it too bright to see beyond them, so I slid open the door, and stepped out onto the faux-grass covered balcony, I couldn't believe it: the sun was shining bright on a warm day. I could hear laughing and playing some three floors below me, on the streets there were people dressed in fine summer clothes, walking around and out to the shore just to the

right of me. I've been here before, when I was young, many times before.
I knew this salty smell of sea air; I knew this warm, cleansing breeze; the subtle aroma of tobacco and alcohol flowing in from the neighboring casino. I remember the first time I ever came here, to this very room. That very moment, I was taken back to a stormy early winter day, the evening skies were fully darkened by heavy clouds that poured the ocean onto my younger self. On my back I carried an over-packed guitar-case of my belongings, not even an umbrella to shield myself from the rain, but here I did find shelter. I was a boy without a home, no family to come back to, just a bus-ticket and some money I'd been saving for school.

I remember a fear that I never felt before, an uncertainty, the loss of the only comforts I had in the world, and yet, the next morning I awoke feeling as I never had before: cleansed, free, and driven. My life was now in my own hands, and I wanted, more than anything, to act, I didn't know how or what exactly, but at that moment, I knew there was a problem, and it was my duty to fix it.

I spent every day between then and my enlistment, working an odd job, traveling to a new state, reading book after book on history and politics during the long bus rides. In a time when every child was told '*go to college*', '*save for college*', I took to investing in myself, because I was the only person I could count on to actually look out for me, to help me achieve my goal. I would learn through genuine experience, and through genuine connection, so much of the true substance which made this life so beautiful, which made this country so beautiful, and in turn, what it was that didn't belong, what was driving us apart, and poisoning our soul. I was coming ever closer to the answer.

But of course the issue of what it is I am doing ***here***. The last thing I can remember is the war, we invaded Pittsburgh.

I remember I was shot, but the boys evacuated me.

I'm either dead or dreaming, as far as afterlives go, there could've been much worse than this; I might even go as far as to call this heaven.

There's not much I imagine I can do from here except wait to see where things go, and with that in tow, I showered up, and dressed myself in a fresh white shirt, and khaki slacks. I've missed this place.

Through me flowed a sensation of renewal as I strode along the sandy boardwalk, as though I were feeling a cool breeze across my body for the very first time. The sun shone so bright, and the world looked so clear, as if every little imperfection and glare in my vision had been polished away. I could breathe so smoothly, the ringing in my ears caused by a lifetime around gunfire was gone.

I saw a young boy playing on the beach with his parents, a tall father carrying his small son on his shoulders, three teenagers chasing each other with water-guns. The sight warmed my heart, but left me with a sense of longing. I leaned up against the boardwalk fence, facing the beach, my suddenly bare feet half in the sand and half on the worn planks of the floor.

"Howdy stranger, you come here often?" A young woman said, leaning next to me.

"You always approach strangers?" I shot back, only half looking at her.

"Rude. I'm just being friendly."

"Yeah, friendly's all I can hope for. There's somewhere I ought to be." I said, realizing this woman's presence was bringing a weight back upon me.

"It's too nice out to be busy. How can you work on a day like this?" She slid a cup of lemonade my way, the cup had a merry red and white carnival striping, as did the paper straw. Her hand was fair and pretty, her nails were painted a bright red.

"I'm working toward something important. I wish I could, but I-. You get what I mean." As I turned to finally face her, she vanished, as if she was never there. I still held the lemonade she brought me, it was very sweet at first, but became bitter the more I drank it, though it did take away the stress I'd felt. I wound up dropping it in the sand half-way through while I continued to watch the waves flow onto the shore.

Chapter 7

Pennsylvania, Philadelphia
February 1 1980
|Del Kirk|

"Lord, give me the wisdom to fulfill this duty I've been entrusted with; may my course stay true, and my actions be sufficient to the needs of those who depend on me. Lord, grant Commander Doctor the vigor and vitality to overcome his condition, show him the path he need follow to once again join us in life. So shall it be done."

We were all worried for the Commander, he'd been in a coma since we evacuated him from Pittsburgh. With Doctor incapacitated, authority fell to me as new acting commander of the military; some were, of course, unhappy with a Texan taking command of what essentially was the army of New England, but the majors could think of no better choice, and so I reluctantly accepted.

We had searched intensely for Bull, but there were no traces of him or even his weapon. Studying the bullets lodged within Doctor's torso confirmed our suspicions that Bull had gone rogue.

We were concerned that Bull would strike again, and finish the Commander off in his weakened state, so for his own safety, we circulated a story that Doctor had died in the hospital. If Doctor recovers, and I hesitantly stress that *'if'*, we will explain the story to the public, but if he fails to awake, it'd be better the public see it as the death it was, and not a drawn out spectacle that loses interest.

The nation was in a mourning anguish the day I gave the announcement; Commander Doctor had been assassinated by rogue-captain Johnny Bull, AKA Garrath King, and I, Major Del Kirk Junior, would be assuming the position of commander to the Amerikan New Order.

Massive shoes were left for me to fill, but I wasn't about to let that discourage me; the public needed to know who I was, and that needed to be a man worthy and capable of completing Doctors mission.

I tried to do as much good as I could behind a closed door, hoping they'd start to judge me based on my actions and the policies I could put into place.

First order of business was making sure all the pieces Doctor had put in motion kept spinning, that meant the occupation in the west, reconstruction of Pennsylvania, and negotiations with the other sovereign states. Much easier said than done.

Gran California, and Great Louisiana were straightforward in their unwillingness to negotiate with a Texan, worried I was plotting to make a greater Texas out of the New Order, at the same time, soldiers in Cascadia territory were pushing for independence because they saw my government as illegitimate; I granted them self governance under Doctor's proposed Confederation map, sending them the details as Doctor wrote them, and managing to keep them in the Union as a commonwealth.

This action inadvertently forced me to initiate the next phase of Western Occupation, which was the reorganization of the territory into four new commonwealths minus Cascadia, introducing the Commonwealth territories of Heartland, Ford, and Superior into the Confederation, giving me the rushed task of overseeing and ensuring that functional governments rose to power in each one, thankfully we accomplished this pretty seamlessly.

Relations did improve with Deseret, and President Smith agreed to unite with us, creating the Deseret Commonwealth.

Our Confederation now isolated Gran California from any neighbor allies, while Great Louisiana's only ally of New Dixie remained friendly to us.

The other Presidents and myself established Doctor's vision of the Commonwealth Council, and held our first meeting as the seven leaders of the New Order; We got along pretty well, though disputes were raised whenever I and President Houston of Texas came to a mutual agreement. I understood I wasn't best fit to represent New England, but for the time, I'm the only one qualified, and I assured everyone who challenged my stance that I would hold New England's best interests at heart.

We came to an agreement of specialization to stimulate the economies of our commonwealths, and produce more necessary resources for each other.

We agreed to prioritize Machinery for Ford, Lumber for Cascadia, Livestock for Texas, Oil for Deseret, Crops for Heartland, Ores for Superior, both Fish and Medicine for New England, since Doctor had planned to divide the region into the New England, and Metro Commonwealths.

Policy, while it made a change, was not enough to show these folks that I intended to do all in my power for them, just as Doctor would've intended.

I decided the best way to make my name and goals known would be to televise a speech, I'd deliver it in Philly to a crowd of our soldiers, and broadcast it along every available channel.

I took the podium, and delivered,
"My fellow Amerikans, I recall sitting in a tavern with my good friend, Jim Stark-" I gestured to Jim in the crowd, and the audience applauded for him. "-we were fortunate to see a Texas independent from the Old Regime, but we knew that so long as it existed, and we in opposition to it, Texas would never truly be independent. We rallied together the men who would become known as Ranger company-" A cheer erupted from the Rangers, and I smiled. "We lent our arms to Doctor so we may combat a shared enemy, one which, I am happy to say, has been defeated for good." The audience let out a roaring cheer. "I recall promising myself, and to my father-" I reflected for a moment. "-I promised I would put an end to the Federal Government's tyranny, and keep these lands, all our lands, freed from parasites and tyrants! I can happily say I have fulfilled that promise. We in Texas, New England, in New Dixie, Great Louisiana, Deseret, and Gran California, are free and secure to pursue whatever future we desire for our people, but as much as it may seem I've reached the end of the rainbow, I've been given a new duty; I promised to Commander Doctor, and his men, that I would carry on his goals to the letter, and I intend on fulfilling that promise." A wave of applause followed. "Commander Doctor had a vision for this nation, and it was his vision alone that brought us to this point of achievement; to steer away now would be foolish, to attempt any reversal would undermine that vision. I intend to act, in my new position of power, just as commander Doctor would have intended to act. There were a number of plans the late Commander left behind, but I will see to it that all are completed." This was met with a long unanimous cheer and applause. "It is in my opinion, and the opinion

of Commander Doctor, that we, the Amerikan people, are stronger united, yet are indisputably distinct from one another. The Commander has left us a solution to this dilemma-"

Behind me clicked on a projection of the current Amerikan map outlined on a white background. There were the six independent, greater states, and the labeled occupied territories.

"This is where we are today. I have been in regular contact with the president of Texas, a good friend of my family, and someone who recognizes the importance of Texan sovereignty, but someone who also recognizes that alone, things are difficult; drinking water is a major issue, skilled labor shortages, and inflation all plague the Free State. Given the choice, we'll happily endure these hardships if it means we remain the kings of our own destiny, but we as Amerikans are brothers, and while your brother need not tell you what to do, they should have your back, and you should have theirs. That is the purpose of this arrangement-" The projection changed to show New England territory, Deseret, and Texas all in red, but in four distinct shades. "I would like to declare on behalf of the people of New England, Texas, Deseret, and the Commonwealths of the occupied zone, our unity in the Confederation of New Amerika." Our soldiers were absolutely ecstatic, shaking hands, and high-fiving soldiers from the volunteer companies. "Under this new order, the states, or rather, *the Commonwealths* of the Confederation, shall retain their current governments, but exist in a military and trade union with one another, preserving our freedom through sovereignty, while preserving our strength through unity." The crowd applauded. "I would like to end my speech with a biblical verse a young-man from Saints company once told me: *I dreamt of a statue, a great statue whose head was made of gold, its chest and arms made of silver, its belly and thighs made of bronze, its legs of iron, and feet of clay. A stone struck the statue at its feet, and brought it crashing down, so the once great statue was but chaff in the wind.* As people mix with one another, so will they hold together no better than gold mixes with clay. I envision a statue of gold, a statue for silver, a statue for bronze, a statue of iron, and a statue of clay, not foolishly amalgamated, but standing side by side; beautiful in their own merit, but even more glorious together."

New York, Bronx
February 1 1980
|Garrath King|

Dr. Levine Yagoda, that was the name of the man who'd sprung me from the fort. He went by the moniker '*Nemo*' as a codename of sorts.

I demanded answers the moment we were comfortably distant from the city. I was prepared to use what force was left in my body and rifle to force an explanation, but he sang his song liberally, insisting that there was no need to keep secrets anymore, and that any enemy of Doctor's was a friend of his.

"I came from Soviet Union-" He had told me. "-arrived in 1953 to a sympathizer I had been in contact with. My contact had ferried me into California where I was provided documentation with which to disappear into American society."

"And somehow you've ended up here? What are you, KGB? Stasi?"

"KGB did not exist by this point. I was briefly associated with MGB, predecessor to KGB. I was appointed to position from young age by *Beria* at request of my father, a doctor for elite Soviet officials."

He'd go on in detail to tell me that he fled the USSR, having run for the hills when his father and numerous other doctors were purged by Stalin; everyone expected that tyrant to die any day, but he didn't, and a new great purge was launched, one which Yagoda knew he'd be in the crosshairs of.

It was here in the states that he once again picked up a job in the government, this time in the CIA, putting the instruction he received in espionage to good use.

Upon our return, the two of us took shelter in the desolate slums of the Bronx; this particular region had been nearly entirely wiped out in a battle between Doctor's men, and an alliance of gangs.

We knew we'd go unnoticed, at least for a little while. We set up shop in an abandoned hospital, it was here that the doc was able to more thoroughly treat my wounds. I was left with an unusable arm, and a crippled leg, confining me to a chair at most times, and a wheeled brace when movement was necessary.

I'd been miserable until I heard the announcement: Doctor was dead, but I soon began to wish I was as well.

"Is there problem, Mr.Bull?" The doc had asked me, noticing I was brooding in my chair again, glaring out the window at the still growing city.

"My fight's done, doc. I don't know what's left for me in this world. I'm a cripple, a wanted man, essentially exiled from my home, and surrounded by the achievements of the man who crippled me. I just want it to end already." I told him.

"Let me tell you story." He pulled up a chair, and sat across from me. "Is 1952, my father does not return home from his work. We are informed of a plot uncovered to assassinate Stalin by poisoning. Several doctors are held responsible, but further yet, the jews are held responsible. My mother fears the worst, and encourages me to flee the country to Israel, many do, but travel becomes forbidden before I am given the opportunity, little did I know I would be the fortunate one. We are in similar situation, but you are prepared so quickly to give up. What if I told you that you could walk once again? I sense in you that your work has only just begun. You have lost much, and while it cannot be restored, you can still take away as much as was taken from you, the only cost would be time and pain."

"Look at me, there's no pride in what I've become, there's no happiness for me beyond this point in my current state. I'll pay that price, doc." I answered, leaving him nodding with a smirk which left me the slightest bit uneasy.

"Very good. This is project I have been developing for long time, an accumulation of Soviet and American ingenuity compiled into a work truly beautiful. I assure you that you will not be displeased."

New York, Neu York
June 5 1980
|Percy Holiday|

"I tell ya, man, from this point forward, our job is nothing but smooth sailing on a breezy summer day." Holden remarked while we finished our patrolling the streets of the city once known as Manhattan.

The once drab, grey structures of the old city were but a thing of the past, in process of being replaced by an architectural styling which Doctor termed '*New Amerikan*', the concept was meant to become the core visual identity in the soon-to-be Metro Commonwealth of Neu York, Connecticut, Boston, Philly, Jersey, Delaware, and Maryland; Doctor envisioned it as a blending of modern art-deco symmetry with the hardy greco-romanesque architecture of colonial America, producing structures which resembled towering, narrow pyramids, obelisks, ancient monuments, and temples, all cut from solid marble stones of black and white, and lined in shimmering gold and silver trimmings.

Reconstruction has only begun relatively recently, just a few years ago, and so, walking through the city was like walking through a massive construction project; small bits of rubble still littered some of the streets in less developed districts; scaffolding formed a never-ending balcony just above the sidewalks.

One of the most impressive projects that had been completed was the new *Outer-city Ring*, a city-round, mass highway system bordered by scenic grasslands, and small, developing roadside communities which brought a slice of the suburbs to the city.

Evergreens and wildlife were reintroduced to the island for the first time in centuries, breathing new life into what was once a monument to soulless structure, and the unnatural.

Holden and I were tasked with basic occupation duty, that being to patrol the city for any trouble while reconstruction continued. Our's was an easy job: No combat, no major oversight, it was just Holden and I overseeing the districts we were appointed to in the mornings, and reporting in at the end of the day.

We had another year left until we were no longer obligated to continue our term, and it seemed the remainder of this term would be served here in the city, which gave us the benefit of exploring and enjoying the place in our free time. The *Outer-city Ring* was a great recreational spot, especially since a lot of the city still wasn't ready for public use. Holden and I would spend our free days in the grasslands, jogging, hitting on chicks when conditions would serve, playing chess, baseball, or whatever the hell. Of course, the job always took precedence; we'd discovered a pair of chicks we'd been speakin' with were secretly commies, unfortunately we have a zero-tolerance policy for it, and they had to go.

Nights were nice, the two of us would go out for bowling, probably finishing off the day by shooting the breeze at the all-night diner, which is where we had just stopped into for dinner.

"Smooth sailing, man." Holden reminded me. "We're basically in our senior year, no serious work left, just seat-time, you know?"

"I guess, Holden. Easy as it might be, we do still have a job to do." I said, reminding him.

"You've been kinda too serious ever since we got here, what's the deal, man?" He asked. The truth was that ever since the Commander died, I've felt like I failed him; I know there was nothing I could have done, but it reminded me just how much this wasn't a game. Holden still wanted to go home, put this behind him, and live life like none of it even happened, this really isn't sticking to him, but that's how he copes with it. Me, this is my life; I can't justify going home to slack-off when I know there's more important things to do.

"I've just been thinking about life, man." I answered.

"Yeah, we all do, but, like, what about life?"

"I feel like I'm meant to do something big, but I don't know what it is. You know, at first, I thought this soldier gig was it, but what's a soldier do when the war's done? I still want to protect people, you know, do my part, but I don't know what that is."

"That's some heavy stuff, man." Holden answered. "If I were you, I'd be a policeman."

"I mean, that's not it entirely, dude. I kinda feel like we've hit a loop, you know, like we're just driving in circles, just doing things but not REALLY going anywhere, and I know, because if we were going somewhere, we'd be feeling something, maybe some kind of fulfillment, or hell, even disappointment, but I really feel like I'm just standing water, going bad."

"Well, I mean-" Holden's answer was cut off when he noticed someone pasting a poster up in an alleyway. "-Now that seems a little out of place."

"You stay here, I'll go check it out." I told him, excusing myself from the table, and rushing to the alley once I was outside.
"Hey, you!" I yelled out, inciting him to run from the scene, and disappear down the alley by the time I had reached it. "Huh." He'd dropped a few posters before he'd taken off. I turned my head to the sign he'd pasted up, feeling a foreboding as I read,

"The Iron Burns RED When Put Under Pressure. Who Is Nemo?".

New York, Bronx
June 20 1980
|Garrath King|

"-I developed close relationship to many within upper echelons of American government-" Nemo told me as he fine-tuned all the widgets and gizmos of my new arm. "-there was one man in particular whom I took a shine to, radical politician with good support from both moderate and extreme left of country, his name escapes me, but regardless, he far lacked support to become president, a shame, I thought if any man had capability to bring this nation to socialism, it was him."

"What is it with you and socialism anyhow?" I asked. "I can understand you being brought up with it, but after the Soviets turned their back on you, I figured you might've had a change of heart." I posed to him. He paused from his tinkering, and reclined back in his chair, hands together.

"Socialism has good intention, but is not perfect system, certainly neither capitalism, however both carry elements which overlap well; inevitably, in both systems you will see the rise of an elite class, despite socialism's best attempts at class elimination. Simple understanding of human evolution dictates that hierarchy will form through nature, therefore leadership is necessary to regulate both systems. In capitalism, the elite are those who can attract and maintain the greatest amount of money, they need not be the best, or even the brightest, simply, one who can exploit luck or strategy can achieve a high enough state in the hierarchy to where his competitors are few; if one who reaches a high rank can become allied to his competitors, monopoly develops, and the top-dogs must only swat away and crush the small-dogs who grow to a threatening size. Capitalist elites, unless they are by chance the best and brightest, will almost always exploit those below them, and even when best and brightest reach high rank, they are likely to be dethroned or outlasted by the cheaters. Now, in socialism, the elite are those best able to attract support of public, and maintain power however necessary. Socialist elites do not allow for opposition to exist and will crush it at first appearance. In both cases, the elite will develop greater self interest over the needs of the people. For men like me, for jews, for any minority or dissident, security and freedom under either cannot be ensured in these systems as they are, and the same goes for Doctor's fascistic government. I believe-" Nemo paused to look at my mechanical arm. "-in an alternative."

New York, Neu York
June 30 1980
|Percy Holiday|

The longer Holden and I stuck around the city locals, the more we realized just how much the war had changed people; pre-war, the city was mostly liberal, lots of minorities too, but the blacks had been entirely segregated to their own district in Harlem, with the region completely encircled by the white districts to prevent any migration out or in, not even we were allowed in there, only black members of our company ran patrols through the district. People got a lot more tribal; separate co-existence kept ethnic tensions non-existent, but any crossover almost always led to extreme violence, hence, why we, even while armed, couldn't patrol what essentially was foreign land.

The smaller minorities of hispanics and asians were in most cases deported or heavily integrated into a second-class role, spread out widely to prevent the creation of any community; however, some remained as underground gangs or syndicates which have succeeded in evading the law for now, though still face another threat more severe than us:

The more greatly tribal white society, specifically the new youth, had adopted an ultra-nationalist identity with an affinity toward brutality; the *Ultras*, as this youth came to be known, organized together in what could best be described as gangs, some even basing themselves off of Bull's gang overseas. These gangs of *Ultras* would make a game out of hunting down, and making examples of ethnic gang members or sympathizers, on occasion utilizing an execution method Doctor's men had developed and abandoned on account of it's cruelty; the practice, first used following the battle of New York, was known as '*Skull Bleaching*', and was intended to induce a terrifying but quick death by dissolving all soft flesh above the neck with a high-powered acid sprayer, but the acid wasn't as strong as previously believed, and the method was decommissioned, still it did it's job of terrifying potential dissidents, nobody wanted to be on the receiving end of that weapon. Some of the *Ultras* had managed to get their hands on the old acid-sprayers, and put them back into use in the underground as both a terror weapon, and a means of torture.

Even amongst each other, some *Ultras* believed in a philosophy of '*culling the herd*', to pit themselves against friends in genuine battles to the death, these individuals were seen as extreme even by other Ultras, but they were, without argument, the most formidable and battle-hardened of the groups, holding most closely Doctor's advocacy of hardship for the sake of growth, and that there is no security in the natural world but your own strength.

These were the kinds of things Holden and I had to investigate and resolve in our time: Territorial crossover, ethnic gangs, *Ultra* gangs, death fights, and now, most recently, the *Red Technate.*

Posters began springing up all about the city. In every district: fliers, criers, and smugglers have been reported, but they've bypassed us at every turn, today, that changed.

"A better society awaits! A fairer society! One of security and progress! Take heed, brothers! Let us embrace a new era in the arms of a force greater than man, and more tangible than god!"

A man in a red shirt and mask was giving his little decree to a crowd of some dozen people, tossing out leaflets from the back of a truck parked in an alley.

"Hey! Stop where you are!" Holden yelled.

"You're in potential violation of sedition law, pal. We're going to need to bring you in for a few questions." I followed up to Holden.

"Oh no, you're not taking me anywhere! I know what ends up to guys like me when they're taken in for '*questions*'!" The speaker declared as he tried backing into the trailer of the truck.

"Calm down, now. We're serious, we just need some information, no funny business." I said attempting to negotiate with him, but to no luck, as a moment later, he called out for the truck driver to pull out of the alley, and take off onto the highway.

"Call it in, Perc, we might be able to get a vehicle on them if we act quick." Holden insisted, but I nodded against it.

"This isn't going to be the last we see of them, they're picking up more steam. Next time we spot a crier like that, no talk, just make the arrest, guns ready." I told him.

"Yes, sir."

New York, Bronx

July 1 1980
|Garrath King|

We'd been faced with another summer rain shower; it brought me comfort to know the rain would drive everyone else to be stuck indoors like myself.

The doc returned from one of his scavenging runs, bringing with him another week's supply of food. He shook off his shoes, and hung up his coat before unpacking his bag.

"How'd it go?" I asked him.

"All went well, my friend. I brought you a gift."

"Is it another book?"

"Yes, but perhaps show little more enthusiasm; I believe you will especially enjoy this one." He said as he walked over to hand me a copy of *The Age Of Revolution by Winston Churchill.* "Is part of larger collection I once read, but I could only find this one at moment." I took the book, analyzing it eagerly.

"I've heard of this series; anytime I tried to pick it up I just couldn't afford it. Thanks, doc."

"Is my pleasure. Always have I held a great admiration for the accomplishments of the English."

"Yeah? That so?" I asked.

"Oh absolutely!" He insisted. "It amazes me how a people confined to so small and disconnected an island as Britain were able to establish so vast an empire, and throughout, combat perhaps history's greatest adversaries."

"Some might say we just got lucky."

"I disagree; against terrible odds, all which should have destroyed your people instead made them stronger. It is not by mere chance that your nation has produced some of history's greatest inventors, leaders, and philosophers. From an island with limited resources, you have achieved more than perhaps the whole of continental Europe in the fields of science, trade, conquest, and discovery. From an island, you alone held dominion across the entire globe, that is truly spectacular."

"That's mighty kind of you, doc, but the empire's gone; we're back to square-one, you might say. I'd argue it'll be a while if ever we could rebuild all we once had."

"So great a shame, your decolonization; it is like stripping a general of his medals or a king of his clothes. You have my condolences, Mr.Bull."

"Heh, never took you for a pro-colonial type, doc, what with all your socialism and such."

"Oh of course! I abhor oppression and subjugation, but I am also a man of reason; I look at Africa, and I see famine, I see violence, primitivism, but upon arrival of the British: Lands which were but underdeveloped jungle now became farms and cities. It is only reasonable that a more developed society adopt underdeveloped societies to nurture and raise properly; does he with knowledge not have an obligation to share that with others to achieve the betterment of the collective human-race? While mistakes were made, I believe more than not that British colonialism achieved more good for the Africans than not."

"Thank you! Heh, if only you could encourage the ***prolies*** back home of that, to them it's always 'colonialism is slavery', and 'there's no excuse for colonialism'. Before we set foot on that damned continent, most 'em didn't even have the bloody wheel! Now look how it is that we pulled out: Bloody miserable!"

"It is part of who you are to educate, rule, and improve. It is unfortunate to say, but most men in this world are incapable of ruling themselves, let alone entire nations, leadership like that which yours offered to others is more precious a commodity than any could imagine."

"Damn straight, gov. No one treated their subjects better than us, we gave the most backward little corners of the world a chance to race past even our European contemporaries, but I say it's their loss."

"Yes, but even if your own corner of world remains bright, how long will it be until the darkness surrounding you ultimately extinguishes your light?" He said, leaving me without answer, and allowing him to continue. "My people too were shaped by hardship, and a necessary focus upon ourselves. Of us have emerged some of the greatest minds of history: Einstein, Freud, Marx, Bohr, Mahler, I could go on. Just like you, our ascension and achievement was berated, and shunned by the masses who resented the advancements nature had gifted upon us; always when we reached a level of power were we forced out, butchered, and slandered, but unlike you, however, we had no sanctuary, no home to call our own, and yet we persevere."

"You can't expect a population of fools to know what's best for them, in most cases you simply need to enforce it, allow their descendants to appreciate what they couldn't."

"Absolutely, it takes time for men to realize what is in their best interest, though force will only achieve so much, and taint the legacy of your actions, myself, I prefer persuasion, of course, persuasion to trigger action, but regardless."

"That's easier said than done, doc. It's a shame how much blood we need to shed to keep civilization on its feet; sometimes I wonder if ever we should've colonized at all, and just protected ourselves instead."

"Never allow yourself to believe that you are to apologize for attempting to make this chaotic world of ours a better place, Mr.Bull. Without intellectual people such as ours, this planet would have remained savage! But there is truth to our woes, there is only so much humans can do, even intellectually adept men cannot secure global prosperity."

Maine, Old Orchard Beach
July 4 1980
|Augustus Doctor|

I recall the last time I was here, it felt as though it'd been centuries. I knew well this wasn't real, yet still things fluxed between the convincingly tangible to the surreal.

It was another warm summer day, the sun shone brightly, and glistened off the water and particles of sand.

I was clothed in an antiquated plated silver armor with golden accents, the armor overlaying a crimson tunic. I wore boots and gloves of brown leather, feeling as though I was delivering a message, and behold, there, clutched in my hand, was a parchment scroll.

My feet guided me to the only other person in sight, a man facing away toward the sea, dressed in white and red robes, like a Roman, he wore a golden wreath crown.

I knelt down on a knee, calling to him as I presented the scroll.

"Commander, I bring you new information from the front-lines. I believe victory to have been drawn."

He turned slowly to face me.

"I believe it is you who requires information from me, young Augustus." His robes were stained red around his chest, partially obscured by the draping fashion of the outfit.

"I hoped to avenge you, Commander. I've championed our cause since the mere age of twenty. Over a decade later, we have achieved all we set out to accomplish."

"Not all, Augustus, there is the matter of your successor."

"Yes, Commander. I delegated authority to my generals, they are to select a successor from among themselves. There are many good men among their ranks who have served long and with valor."

"This will not do, Augustus." He said to my alarm. "I did not select you to assume your role based on your seniority, or even your capability at the time. I selected you because of your potential, your sheer will to power, and how much you understood what the party needed without ever needing to compromise yourself. The party was meant for men like you, and you were meant to lead the party."
He waved his hand, bringing us to the scene of an office, Dirk sat at a desk, enduring criticism and confusion from his cabinet.
"The Texan is a good man, an excellent leader, but not right for New England, and not the face of New Amerika. His war and his cause may share the steps of ours, but it will ultimately lead him elsewhere."

"I understand, Commander. My work then, is not yet done."

"No it is not, far from it. Nemo is still out there, Augustus, he and that Judas, Bull. Traitors and assassins, the two of them. The only rightful punishment for a traitor is death. You may not rest until both are stiffly in a grave, but first you have an heir to secure; A young man like yourself, one not born into luxury or comfort, one whose heart knows only New England and Amerika. You know of one already. Awake, Augustus. Awake and prepare for him all that he will need."

New York, Bronx
September 12 1980
|Garrath King|

The mechanical arm that Nemo built for me was working splendidly, I could perform complex hand movements, grip more tightly than I ever had, and best of all, properly carry my rifle again.

As delighted as I was to regain total function of my upper body, my leg still left me chair-bound. The doc told me that syncing the arm's movements to the muscles in my shoulder were a simple enough task, but a functioning mechanical leg would require a more extensive network, likely a spinal augmentation. I was afraid as Nemo told me spinal work could leave both my legs paralyzed, or even worse.

The more I grew used to my new arm, the more the idea of a new leg appealed to me, regardless of the risk. I thought the surgery to be a proper gamble, as without one leg, I couldn't rightly use the other anyhow, and if it succeeded-

"I have returned with more machinery." Nemo announced as he shut the door behind him, dropping a heavy cardboard box of metal on the ground next to a number of monitors he'd been tinkering with. "I had very busy day, Mr.Bull, but I believe fortune may be shining upon us yet."

"Yeah? What makes you say that?" I wondered.

"The seeds of dissent which I have planted are beginning to sprout into a lovely flower of revolution."

"Heh, yeah, good luck with that. Most every liberal and commie in the city willing to take up arms was executed years ago. I don't imagine you'll be able to grow as much as a protest." I told him.

"Hm, perhaps, but perhaps not. Tell me, have I ever told you the story of how the war began?"

"Not entirely, no."

"Yes, you recall my mentioning of a particular politician whom I took interest in? I had, over a number of years, groomed not only this man, but a number of men to assume positions as vice-presidents. Presidency was simply out of question, I could not groom a successful socialist President without forcing him to blatantly lie to public, but as vice-president, the possibility to assume power existed, better yet, many took place in other institutions from congress to the court. I then, through multiple means of influence, brought major candidates of Republican party and Democrat party to adopt my agents as their vice presidents. Thankfully, the politician I especially liked had replaced previous vice-president choice of Mr.Kennedy, who then went on to win election."

"How fortunate then that he'd be assassinated." I commented.

"Fortune, Mr.Bull, is but a word which to me has come to mean my own actions."

"What do you mean?"

"One cannot rely upon luck alone to carry his agenda forward; however, it is sometimes in one's interest to act as if it has. I was not simply going to hope my agent would succeed the president, I was necessary to make it happen."

"Are you saying that you shot the president?"

"Political assassination was one of earliest lessons in MGB, to silence opposition or dissident, but to also create cloud of confusion around deaths of major targets, especially politicians. My agents had spread out widely into the political machines of American government, and now, gradually, we would turn up heat for American public."

"Well geez, doc. Now that seems downright sinister of you."

"No change in this world ever comes cleanly, Mr.Bull. There is a reason why change takes time, and why it exists. There are many who are content simply to live within a broken system, and few who are willing to do what is necessary for the betterment of more than himself." He looked at my arm again. "Which reminds me, if we are to better your leg, we will need to follow a more extreme procedure. I can procure all necessary components within a week if you are willing, but I need a decision now."

"I suppose I do want to, doc, I'm just a bit scared, as pathetic as it may sound."

"Fear is often what holds back men from doing what is necessary. I too feared fleeing the USSR, and while for the moment I was comfortable, I knew if I stayed, death would follow. Many jews of USSR fled to Israel, and adopted a false sense of security, not realizing how large a target the state had been laid surrounded by Soviet-sympathetic Islamic nations, while daring to align itself with the US; we should have seen the invasion coming, but I don't believe any expected Stalin to lend full support to Egypt. Israel fell, and those who weren't massacred gained asylum in Britain and France."

"Goddamn Hajji's. I didn't realize, mate. I'm sorry to hear."

"Pity me not, for my goal leaves me without fear. I only ask the same of you; our goals overlap, and there is much we can do in support of each other, but you will need your legs. Are you ready to walk again, Mr.Bull?"

New York, Neu York
December 20 1980

|Percy Holiday|

Reports had begun coming in from other cities in the occupancy zones of Philly, Maryland, Delaware, and Jersey, all describing the same activities we've associated with the *Red Technate.*

From interrogations and investigations, we've figured out that they are some type of socialist group with an agenda of absolute equalization, and mechanical revolution.

With the Commander gone, socialists have secretly resurged and rallied under the Technate banner. As it turned out, what we faced on the battlefield was mostly supplanted by soldiers of the Old Order, while a lot of the extreme-left had just waited for one side to eliminate the other, and leave itself weakened for conquest. Again, with the Commander gone, they felt now was their chance.

I led a squad to bust up a den of commies over in Queens, it felt like we were once again at war. We found that the hideout we'd raided had what most of the criers tended to carry in those trucks of theirs: Fliers, posters, and on occasion we'd find a stash of makeshift or illegal firearms. One item of interest we managed to gather was a Technate map, showing us the distribution of their men, and just how far their ambitions stretched.

"They're aiming to capture the entire Metro Commonwealth territory." I dictated to the room of patrol soldiers back at basecamp. A large projection of the captured map was blown up on the wall. "They're calling it the Megalopolis, or Red Technate, they want to capture major North Eastern cities under reconstruction, and unite them into one mass, industrial, urban state. The Technate, as the name implies, is meant to be initially run by scientists and intellectuals, but the goal is to eventually completely automate governance." The projection changed to an expanded map that reached out deeper into the Commonwealths. "We assume cities will only be the first phase of their plan. In order to achieve relative self-sufficiency, they will require resources from these regions here; much of New England, Ford, and even Canada could see invasion by the Red Technate. Our best hope of defeating this menace is by hunting down the group's leadership." The projection now showed a poster which read '*Who is Nemo*'. "This is likely our man. He escaped the battle of Pittsburgh, and is likely to be in one of these major cities, ours included. I've put the word out to our men in the Metro area; we find this man-" A projection now showing our only photo of Nemo clicked on. "-and we bring down the Red Technate."

New York, Bronx
January 1 1981
|Garrath King|

The doc's procedures had paid off; I could stand, I could walk. I felt a strength beneath me which I had never felt before. I was absolutely delighted. I just wanted to run outside, but Nemo discouraged it, insisted we were still in hiding. The doc made good of disguises whenever he left to scavenge, but he argued I'd stick out like a sore thumb.

I really began to wonder about what it was the doc had been working on this whole time. Being chair-bound, I spent most of my time just staring out the window or reading a book that the doc would bring me from one of his expeditions, but I didn't ask much about his project, frankly, 'just seemed like he was hooking up a television system of sorts, but roaming around the hospital, I found the wires, monitors, and machinery extended all throughout the halls in what looked like the inside of a massive computer.

"Hey doc!" I called out. "What is all this? Didn't realize how extensive this project of yours was." He stepped into the hall from another room.

"I realized years ago that man, with all his flaws, will always abuse his power, will always push against equality for his own benefit. We require leadership, but man is unfit to govern other men, that is why I developed this-" The monitors suddenly came alive, showing across ten screens some hundred feeds, not just in the hospital, but across the city.

"What in the hell-" I said as the video-feeds split into hundreds that the eye could hardly read. Suddenly the images vanished, and were replaced by one continuous red line.

"-I call it, *Odin*." Nemo said.

"*Hello, Dr.Yagoda.*" The machine spoke in a voice that echoed throughout the hospital, the red-line fluctuating as it did. "*Hello, Garrath King.*"

The doc turned the device off.

"This is just the beginning, Mr.Bull. Odin has eyes all throughout the city, more importantly, it can understand what it sees, but-!" Nemo once again looked at my metal arm, and now at my leg. "-Odin is but a brain, a brain without a body."

"*I look forward to working with you, Garrath King.*" I suddenly heard echo in my head.

"What! What was that!?" I demanded, alarmed.

"Relax, Mr.Bull. Your spinal augmentation has direct wireless connection to Odin's operating system. He can speak to you, and you can speak to him, you can know what he knows, see what he sees." In that moment, I saw live surveillance from all around the city. I saw as if my eyes were the camera, I knew their exact location, that of the cameras. I could identify people and things.

"W-Why, doc? Why would you do this?" I said with a shake in my voice, and a trembling body.

"There is no need for alarm, Mr.Bull. I told you we could stand to benefit each other, to help each other achieve our goals. I have given you capabilities that make you perhaps one of the most powerful men on the planet."

"I-I don't know, doc. I'm not sure I can handle this."

"Mr.Bull, please, listen to me, you've been forced from your home, betrayed, seen countless of your men die for a tyrant, and now his legacy shines brightly atop the corpses of your people. You can choose to return home, you are more than capable of using Odin to navigate yourself to a safe vessel, and operate it using Odin's extensive information database. Once you reach one hundred miles distance, signal will be lost, and Odin's voice will disappear. Alternatively, you use this gift to strike back at Doctor, taking all that mattered to him, as he has taken from you. Will you be Odin's hand, will you act, or will you run?"

New York, Neu York
June 4 1981
|Percy Holiday|

Holden was packing up his belongings in the barracks, two years had seemingly passed so quickly. So much has changed for me, rather, so much of me has changed, but not Holden, he was still the same old fella on the inside.

It was such a nice breezy night out that we propped the door open, and lifted up all the windows, filling the barracks with a cool summer wind.

Most everyone was in the cafeteria, but Holden was eager to see Rockport again, packing like tomorrow was the first day of the rest of his life.

"Gettin' out right in time for summer, Perc!" Holden was laughing, nearly singing every word. "Finally goin' home, man! Ain't you excited!" He happily punched me in the arm, but soon sensed I wasn't as enthusiastic as he was. "Guess not, huh? I kinda figured it'd be like that. I just hoped different."

"What do you mean?" I asked.

"I mean, you've gotten real serious, Perc. I remember we first walked into this gig, you just wanted to get home, now it feels like that don't even matter to you anymore."

"It still matters to me, man, but I've got work to do, this job's important."

"Hell, I know it is! Not just for everyone else, but you've really found your place here, man, and that's terrific. I don't want to take it away from you, I just wish it wasn't splitting us apart like it has." I tried to argue against it, but he cut me off immediately. "You know it has, man. I don't hold it against you, I just miss how things used to be. I know you look down on me, man. You probably know I think this job's for stiffs. I get it, the way I talk, I'm always fixated on right now, I don't even have a job set for when I get back. I don't know where we're all gonna go, but I know that we'll get there. What's always been important to me is my family, that's you and Tyler, you two are all I got. I just want to go home, it's all I wanted from day one. You found something better, and as much as I'm gonna miss you, you've got to pursue it, you hear? I liked teaching you to be tough and all, but you're a man now, you don't need that kinda talk no more. I've still got a bit of kid left in me, so I'm gonna enjoy it one last time." He paused for a moment to think back. "I remember how I thought, back in town-hall that night, that one day things might not be how they used to, that eventually the games needed to end, that the time would run out, and I guess that's what this is, where we are right now, end of the line. But I can say that I never regretted a day of it. We spent all the days we had, but we lived the hell outta them." He put his hand on my shoulder, and smiled. “Thanks for keepin’ us safe so that we can keep livin’ like we do.” He gave me a tight hug. “I love you, man.” He gave me a hard pat on the back, picked up his bag, and made for the door, turning around to see me one more time. “Don’t die on us, Percy. Tyler and me are gonna expect you home one day. Don’t let us down.”

He left. I kinda just stood there, my head fog disappeared and I realized I was on my own.

I climbed up to the watchtower, from there I could see Holden’s tail-lights on the slow highway, my eyes followed them until they reached the bridge, and disappeared as he crossed into Jersey. I continued to stare into the distance where his car once was.

My thoughts were teetering between reminiscing over the memories of my friends, and a relief of being alone to focus on my work. I wasn’t fully sure what this meant, but whatever the case, this is my reality now, and I needed to make the best of it.

I climbed back down, and caught up to my teammates in the cafeteria, serving myself some food, and taking a seat fairly away from everyone else, but that didn’t stop one soldier from asking,

“Hey Captain, is everything alright?”

Before I could answer, every light in the camp went dark. A groaning ‘boom’ sounded from a distance away, and suddenly we heard over our loud-speakers, and echoing throughout the city, a distorted voice,

“Doctor’s people-” It paused. “-your reckoning is at hand.”

Chapter 8
New York, Kingston
June 5 1981
|Del Kirk|

I paced hard down the halls of the old hospital.

The situation in the Metro territory had rapidly spread from Neu York to other major cities in the span of only a few hours. I called in support from Ford and New Dixie, they'd be able to help alleviate the risings in the south and west, but Philly, Boston, Newark, and Neu York were all on us to handle.

There was a total communication blackout from Neu York and Newark, but news from Philly confirmed our suspicions about this *Red Technate* organization; discovered excavated weapon stashes, coordination maps, and tactics observations all led us to believe this had been planned since pre-war, a dormant organization hiding right in plain sight. This seeming betrayal leads me to wonder if we in fact had been too generous in our inquisition. It's like the Commander said, '*every threat we fail to address today equals countless more for tomorrow*.' I felt a deep confliction, I could sense wrath kindling it's flames from within me at the thought of this treachery, but I would not succumb to it.

"Commander Kirk, he's ready to see you now." A physician said, guiding me past a secured door into a medical room. "I'll allow you two to speak privately." The physician said, excusing himself.

"Commander Doctor." I said, saluting the man dressed in red and white pin-striped slacks, and wearing that blue vest.

"Commander Dirk-" He answered, saluting back to me. "-it's good to see you again, old friend."

"The feelin's mutual, sir, though I wish it were under better circumstances." The Commander shot me a serious look of concern.

"What's happened since I've been away?" He asked me.

No later than after I'd informed him of the risings and crisis did he march the both of us out of that hospital and to the army base, from where he'd put in urgent calls to any and all reserve, out-stationed, or occupational forces who could be redirected to eradicate the insurgencies. It seemed as though every call concluded with "Yes! This is Commander Doctor, and I'm very much alive!" Hanging up the line, the Commander turned to me.

"Regional militias and freed Divisions are moving in to support our boys in Boston. I called in a redirection of soldiers from Philly into Newark. New Dixie can handle Philly when they get to it, right now we need to focus on breaching Neu York, we'll charge through Newark, and route troops up into New Haven when the previous two are under control. Now, we need a means of us two reaching the city fast, and with enough armor and firepower to rocket through anything that gets in our way."

"I think I have precisely the thing, Commander."

New York, Grand Central Station
June 5 1981
|Garrath King|

This place was abandoned, well, empty at least. Doctor had collapsed the metro tunnels, but kept the station standing as he'd done with any monuments he considered worth preserving. This left what I'd always imagined a bustling terminal to echo only the footsteps of myself and the Doc Nemo.

The Doc had put me to work sabotaging major power facilities across the island and in other major cities, linking them up to his core Odin system, suffice to say I was thrilled to be back in action again, and happy to find my mechanical implants hadn't heavily impeded my stealth abilities. I'd taken to hindering Doctor's forces by looting and destroying armories and communication lines, supplementing whatever was useful to our own men, oh how I was delighted to have an army again, one I took to training with due haste for this precise battle. I was confident we'd be able to secure the Metro area, from then on it didn't concern me; Doctor's new empire would be toppled, and I could return home to tend to my own.

"What is it we are here for?" I asked, following the Doc's lead, and surveying the area. It felt almost dreamlike, the isolated, removed atmosphere contrasted with the distant battle raging almost softly away from where we were.

"We are here-" Nemo began. "-to *set up shop*, as expression goes." The Doc was seemingly sizing the area up, checking the doors and all.

"Set up shop? Here? Why here of all places?"

"Ah, is not location itself which is valuable, you see, but what lies underneath it. If you follow me, I will explain."
He led us into a concealed elevator shaft, and continued speaking. "Many years ago, when terminal was first built, considerations were made for where to place power generators. City did not want space being wasted upon an accessory to terminal, so instead, terminal tunneled many stories below, and stores generators here. Between generators and surface lies ten stories of shops and storerooms to produce and store all manner of machinery and material for maintenance of generators, trains, and terminal itself, in essence, we have a self-sufficient base of operation to provide us both power and resources, but that is not all. When Cold War broke out, US developed-" He paused. "-well, I will just show you." As the elevator passed floor after floor of gated warehouse rooms, we finally came upon the final subbasement. Nemo slid open the doors and gestured me into the room. "Behold. You may say hello to former Agency of National Security." He said as I came upon a room lined with screens broadcasting surveillance footage from all across the city and beyond.

"Er, hello Agency of National Security." I said with a moment of confusion. Nemo just laughed.

"Mr.Bull, these computers cannot speak like Odin can, apologies for my misspeaking. This display grants us vision across every major city in the North East: New Haven, Boston, Philadelphia, the list goes on, but, system is limited, it can only show so much at a time, and only so many places, but, its network is extensive enough to easily build off of. With additional construction, and addition of my device, we can take this information, and process it at a speed and efficiency no mere human could do with millions of these monitors. We will be able to see all within our new domain, and with Odin, we will know all at any given time. With it, we can eliminate any threats to our new order before they have even begun, identify dissidents, resolve problems with the efficiency human society so direly lacks."

In a moment of lucidity, past the blinders of my desire for revenge, I began to feel a pattern; I felt the same sense of uncertainty I first felt toward Doctor during the *battle of New York*, an uncertainty which I time and time again tucked away, not realizing how deep I was sinking myself into someone else's crusade. I wasn't prepared to invest myself in this once again.

"I'm not on board, Doc."

"Excuse me?"

"I've helped you come this far out of thanks for your support, and in part a desire for revenge, but I've decided I'm no longer interested in this arrangement. You told me I had a choice. I've lost a lot, but I still have something to come home to. I've allowed retribution to blind me to what's good. I'll never see this place again, I just don't give enough of a toss about it anymore, I only want to go home."

"We've already begun our work, Mr.Bull, you can't leave before our work is done!"

"Watch me."

I pushed the Doc aside, but before I could reach the door, he'd shouted something in Russian.

Suddenly, my legs froze in place, and a crushing pain consumed my body.

"Your mind may be rebellious, but that metal in your body belongs to Odin, and Odin belongs to me. You ***will*** carry out our directives."

I groaned in agony. "Why! What've you done to me?!"

"I did more than simply restore your mobility, Mr.Bull. Do you not feel the greater strength in your body? Piece by piece, I was forced to replace bone with metal to ensure you could function. You might even say that below the skin, you are more machine than man. I'd hoped to preserve a mind as agile as yours while improving upon all else, but I considered the possibility of rebellion."

"You can't do this to me!"

"Mr.Bull, you don't understand. Your sacrifice will ensure the security and equality of millions, perhaps billions in the distant future."

"I've heard it all before! I don't want any of it! I just want to feel the soil of my land below my feet again!"

"I cannot allow you to abandon our mission before it has concluded. We cannot bring about civility without eliminating it's enemies, those who stand to abuse, hate, and exploit."

"You're a sick, twisted man, Nemo! Just look at yourself! You denounce the evils of your contemporaries, preaching equality and peace, yet here you are, just another elite trying to force his way on another people. You're an exploiter! You're a parasite!"

"I am a visionary! Compromises are necessary to achieve success, Mr.Bull! Through my own vision, we now have a means to just and unbiased leadership! We will create a society of equality so wars like this need never be fought, so men will never again need to be exploited."

"You're wrong!" I shouted. "When I arrived here, I saw firsthand the degrees of strife between these people, they cannot coexist happily, no matter how much you force them! Perhaps you can force an equal outcome, and preserve peace, but the toll and cost will be immense! You must rob the great to bolster the poor, cripple the strong to empower the weak, destroy what is beautiful to protect the ugly, what is that if not exploitation for your own twisted sense of righteousness, this delusional fantasy of perfect utopia?" He glared at me for a moment. "This world can never be perfect. You and Doctor are both monsters, killing half a population to protect the other! The only difference is that Doctor's society is natural, it may not be paradise, but it is as nature intended. No creature can feel security or satisfaction when it's surrounded by that which at a natural level it knows to be unlike itself, it builds alienation, resentment-" That was when it clicked for me. "That's why, isn't it? You're insecure, unsatisfied, alienated, resentful. You'd want to make everyone as grey and alone as you are, because you don't belong here, you don't belong anywhere." For the first time ever, I watched his face contort into an expression of angered misery; I couldn't help but snicker at my brief victory before he shocked me into unconsciousness. In my last moment of consciousness I heard:

"You cannot understand, Mr.Bull. My life and desires no longer matter, all that matters now is Odin. From here shall emerge a new world order of unity, equality, and prosperity. No man alive can stop us now."

New York, Neu York
June 5 1981
|Percy Holiday|

Power's been cut to major areas; the Reds have taken a great deal of the East-Side. The *Outer-City Ring* is holding out, but won't last long without military support.

We, my men and I, fortified the perimeter of our encampment in the south of Central Park, trying to create a barricade along sixth and seventh avenue to contain the Reds. The Upper East Side is a total liability, locked between Red territory and the Black district, it was hard to secure, but necessary to prevent a northern front if the Reds started leaking into the park.

I'd attempted to coordinate a lock-in between my men and the North-East *Outer-City Ring* to capture the fifty-ninth street border, but communication has been difficult without electricity.

We'd considered reaching out to the black district to occupy the UES, but decided neither of us would be willing to breach the race-border. They were facing their own insurrection, and had no intention in helping their rebels by compromising the border gate.

Every hour of this uprising costs us precious landmarks, and innocent lives. For the sake of everyone on the island, I cannot allow those Bolsheviks to spread any farther. I only wish I had the manpower necessary to properly push into their territory.

As it stood, we were facing an onslaught on our southern border, wave after wave of gun and grenade toting opponents, like a murderous flood.

We were forced to set the streets ablaze to deter the crowd which must have grown to tens of thousands in size; suiciders still charged into the several foot tall flames, firing their weapons for as long as they could, or attempting to carry an explosive through the fire.

Smoke and pulverized cement filled the air, the illumination of the fire giving the smoke all around us a ghastly yellowish-orange color, like the apocalypse was upon us, like the distinction between our world and hell was fading hour by hour.

Shrieks and moans of horrific pain from both sides chilled my skin, and wretched my guts.

Corpses in the fire created a revolting stench that permeated the air, and stuck to everything.

If only every bullet killed; at times it seemed the surviving injured endured a worse fate than the dead: Mangled, eviscerated, in agony until death finally came.

We'd held out for hours, as did they, but just as things seemed their bleakest, that was when salvation finally arrived.

That machine with the body and speed of a sports car, combined with the armor and treads of a tank, maneuvered around our barricade, engine roaring so loud it seemed the air was quaking. The monster of a vehicle blazed through the inferno, spinning a rotary gun latched to it's roof, mowing down row and row of Reds, only ceasing when it's canisters of ammunition finally ran out in the span of what must've been minutes.

We couldn't see beyond the raging flames, but the eruption of that engine followed by hard thuds told us all we needed to know.

At times we saw it emerge from the fire, carrying on it a newly charred corpse, or even multiple at a time.

Soon the harshness of the carnage died to a quiet lull. I ordered my men to extinguish the fires, dousing them in gallons of dirt or water.

A pair of headlights shone through the smoke, and my men cleared the path for the car to come through; out strode two men in hardened armor, leaving not a spot of skin exposed, their shoulders draped in bandoliers of ammo, and shotguns in hand.

"Captain Holiday-" One spoke through a muffling respirator in an all too familiar voice. "-congratulations on your promotion." He saluted me.

"T-Thank you, sir! My god-. Commander Doctor, is that you?"

"The grave can't bind Amerika, Holiday. I am Amerika, Amerika is me, that doesn't change until my work is done." Doctor answered.

"You've done well preserving the island, Percy." Dirk told me, identifying himself. "We have a reinforcement party approaching from the North and West, they'll be approximately five hours out, but still need to capture Newark before advancing on the island. For now, we've got to migrate all able bodied men to the border to reinforce our claim to the territory."

"Communication is down all across the island, only the Reds have access." I replied.

"They must have access to a personal generator-" Doctor added. "-best bet is Grand Central, it's the only one on the East Side. We'll need to regroup our best men to forty-second street, make a direct push across the avenues, it's close enough for a speedy team to capture; if we take it, we'll be able to restore power to parts of the island, and cripple their communications."

"Then we have no time to lose." One of my soldiers commented, but before we could act, a sniper-shot blasted off his face right before us.

Aghast, we turned to the sight of an armored behemoth carrying with him a long rifle; his metal plating made him shine bright in the light of the remaining fires, like a pillaging knight at the site of a burning village. He set his sight on Doctor's tank of a vehicle, putting his hand to it.

"***I thought I heard my car.***" His voice echoed out like a distorted machine.

"Bull?" I asked in shock.

"***Pikey.***" He responded. Without warning, and with the speed of a hummingbird, he took aim again, shooting for me.

I was saved in the nick of time by Dirk who warned us away.

"Commander, take Percy, and get the hell out of here! I'll catch up with you boys!" Dirk yelled out before Doctor directed me to cover. My men retreated close behind.

"***Commander?***" I heard Bull mutter.

New York, Neu York
June 5 1981
|Del Kirk|

"***Commander?***" Bull questioned what he'd just heard, leaving him blind to the hail of slugs I discharged into his side.

He staggered, armor indented deep, but unharmed. He stomped his heavy foot back on the ground violently to regain his balance.

Bull discarded his rifle, and unsheathed from his arms two blades.

"***Nothing personal, gov.***"

I lowered my barrel.

"We don't need to do this, Garrath! This is our choice! We best just walk away!"

"I can't do that, Del."

"This won't end well for either of us, you know that as well as I do. Please, Garrath, we're sons of the same army. You're my brother."

"***We are not brothers!***" He roared scornfully.

"God won't let you take our land, and neither will I." Shells dropped from my shotgun as I reloaded and recocked.

He came in charging like a train, his rapid but weighted metal steps almost crushing the ground beneath him as he drove forward, barely deterred by my fire.

His armor was harder and heavier than anything a man could carry, even a man of his size. Still he moved as if it were nothing, and it was upon my first dodge that I realized the extent of his strength, digging his blade far into the metal barrier behind me, and slicing through it as though it were paper.

He cut a sharp sliver from the wall, and hurled it at me like a javelin, nearly taking my head off.

Rebounding, I closed much of our distance, firing point blank, slug after slug into his chest until cleanly I could make-out a gaping hollow. The fight, in my mind, was finished, and for a brief second I calmed, yet my heart stopped when my gun was grabbed and crushed while still in my hand, revealing past my barrel and in the crater of Bull's chest, not a bleeding wound, but a mess of sparks and dangling wires.

"***There's nothing left***-" Bull groaned through a warped speaker, a blue-light on the side of his face flashing violently. He knocked me to the ground with the remnants of my shotgun, impacting my chest so hard that the air escaped my lungs, and my ribs compressed in a disgusting crackling sound. "***What was that you said about stopping me?***" There was agony in his voice, through the machinery. His body and mind were in pain. More than pain, I could sense fatigue, the tiredness of a man clinging to something he knows is gone, but I wasn't finished. I stood tall despite the pain across my chest.

"What's happened to you, Garrath? What've they made of you?"

"I just wanted things to be as they were. He took more and more of me until there was nothing left but this-" Bull looked down at his metal husk of a body. "-shell." He collapsed forward onto one knee, his injury crippling his functions. "I just wanted to see my home one last time." I felt an aching pity for my old friend.

"I can fix this, Garrath. I can try." I approached him, placing a hand on his shoulder. "There's still salvation for you, brother." It was in that moment I noticed his grip on the metal shard had tightened, as though he were prepared to strike me. He must've seen the disappointment in my face, for instead of slaying me, his grip on the metal loosened until it dropped from his hand with a clink.

"I'm too far gone, Del. You'd best put me out of my misery." He pulled my revolver from its holster and handed it to me. "Will you do me one kindness and take me by the sea, the coasts always took me back to my youth. I used to close my eyes and pretend for a moment I was back where I belonged. I don't think it likely I'll be fortunate enough to fulfill that fantasy, but I can still pretend."

"I'll do you one better, brother." I offered my arm to help him stand. He didn't seem to understand, but took my lead regardless. We half carried each other toward the docks, both slown by our injuries. Along our journey through the ruins of the city I chanted proudly, feeling optimistic for not only myself, but for Garrath as well. "*Amazing grace. How sweet the sound. That saved a wretch like me-.*"

New York, Neu York
June 5 1981
|Percy Holiday|

"Time's come, gentlemen!" Doctor called out, arming his rifle. "We've got a field to reap, and the crop is freedom from the dying grips of the unnatural socialists!" We threw him a roaring cheer of affirmation.

"We've got one target, we're gonna hit it with everything this squad has!" I added, moving to Doctor's side. "Grand Central is no doubt teaming with security forces, expect dense enemy concentration. Make use of incendiaries and explosives, smoke them out into the open, then mow them down. Crowds are easy targets, individuals are easy targets, be prepared to take on both!" To me, my men gave a unified 'Yes sir!'. "Now everyone to muster stations! Arm-up, gear-up, say your prayers, prepare for the worst, know that after this lies a future more beautiful than any of us can imagine, don't hope to see it, hope only to make it so!" They erupted in an impassioned hurrah, chanting my name before vacating to the armory.

I was prepared to dismiss myself, and join my men in the armory, when suddenly Doctor held me by the shoulder.

"Holiday, may I have a word?"

"Yes, Commander."

"I haven't seen another man rally such passion and dedication from a crowd like that in years. They truly look up to you. I wish I had been around to see it all, but you've really come a long way, boy, Captain, rather."

"Thank you, sir. I'm honored."

"That's not all, Holiday. You made a good point, this battle will be intense, we can't hope to see what comes after it, we don't have the right. Before the accident, I'd been thinking about the future; I've been thinking about a succession line, Holiday, finding the right person to lead the Commonwealth after I'm gone. Dirk assuming the role of New England Commander wasn't the best course of action; it was necessary, I know, but a better plan should've been in place. Whoever succeeds me should be someone who understands and values the land as his own home. He should be the best and strongest example of a New England man, to inspire and guide other New England men to be good soldiers and citizens, so that a new leader can be drawn time and time again, always improving; a tribe leader who is the best and strongest of his tribe." Doctor looked right at me. "I want you to be my successor, Holiday, should anything befall me." Doctor said very plainly before continuing.
"You set a high standard for yourself; you cherish your home, your way of life, like a true leader should. In such a short span of time, I've seen what was aimless potential form into a master of his own destiny. I can't think of a better alternative."

"S-Sir, I'm not a politician-" I stammered.

"No one is a politician, Holiday; you think I went to college for it? Think I was born into a political family? I came into this the same way you did, I served my country, I knew what I wanted to fight for, and I never stopped. Those types who call themselves politicians, who seek it as a career, they're nothing more than followers trying to act like leaders. A leader is a man who knows what he wants for himself and his people. His ideas inspire others, and he can show them how to achieve those ideas. You're young, Holiday, you've still got a lot to learn, sure, but life doesn't wait for you to learn, you've got to hop right into the field, and learn as you go along. It's what you've been doing this whole time." He smiled, seemingly reflecting on his own trials and errors. "Life'll throw a lot of wrenches into your plans, but you've got to keep moving. I certainly did." I was, for a moment, speechless, but then he continued, "I want you to promise-" He noticed I was looking away in thought. "Look at me. I know you've got greatness in you. I want you to promise that if anything happens to me, you'll do what's right for New England, for the New Order, and for Amerika. Do I make myself clear?"

"Yes sir." I answered.

We readied ourselves for battle, gathering our soldiers at forty-second street right on our border, beyond this was five long avenues of enemy territory. We'd took precautions to have eyes facing in every direction. Our worst fear was our forces being whittled down before we'd even reached the terminal.

We saw attacks from on high in the scaffolding, emerging from camouflaged hiding spots to blast us with fire and gunshot, but we held tightly, backing one another, our medic ready at a moment's notice to tend a wound or patch a hole.

As the enemy's numbers grew the deeper we moved, Doctor commanded controlled-chaos strategy; groups of two fanned out in all directions to encircle, and secure the perimeter of the target location. The terminal was but minutes away.

Doctor signaled us to halt once in position, we held sights on the target. A substantial count of men and weaponry standing guard outside the building. We radioed Doctor for commands.

"The five machine gunners are going to be our first priority, failing to take them out will make a head-on assault near impossible; all snipers ready?"

"Yes sir, but we only have three snipers, we'll need to take out three, then manage two more before they go on alert, and open fire."

"Simple enough, fire on my-" Our attention was all caught by a loud, mechanical creaking. The machine gunners were directing themselves toward all our positions. "-how!?" Doctor called out, only then realizing the seemingly derelict surveillance cameras watching every one of our groups. "Everyone down!" A torrent of bullets exploded in all directions above our heads.

"*Privyet, Doctor.*" A voice called out from our radios. "*I must say I am impressed for you to have come so far, but in truth, I expected no less. I am aware of your plan, allow me to tell you that it will not succeed. As we speak, my revolutionaries are closing in on your positions. There is no escape. Perhaps you will kill several, but we far outnumber you, my men know this is war of survival, defeat means death; they have nothing to lose, Doctor.*"

The commander shouted in rage, smashing his radio to the ground before turning to me.

"This is bad, Holiday. Even if we get out of here, there's no taking out those gunners. If we had reinforcements to call in, maybe then-" He sighed. "It'll take too long. This is all we got, Holiday, a last stand." We heard voices and heavy steps approaching our location. "It's been an honor serving with you, Captain Holiday."

We primed our weapons, the Commander clasped a grenade, hurling it down the alleyway as we saw the enemy turn into the corner.

Our only exit remained a roaring barrage of bullets. Doctor handed me a mirror to check for an opening, covering his back while the enemy drew closer foot by foot. I heard him grunt in pain.

"Holiday, look out!" I was forced deeper into the alleyway by a molotov that coated the end of the alley in fire.

I took up my gun, contributing to Doctor's fire upon the Reds. The two of us were subject to repeated bullet impacts, fearing each time that this would be the one to kill us. My armor had been penetrated along the side of my leg and near my neck.

They advanced, and we, seeing no means of escape, advanced as well, grenading, reloading, coming ever closer to our opponents whose numbers seemed unending.

Behind us, I heard the machine-gun open fire again, but no longer impacting the alley wall, it was firing off something metal, something that was roaring closer with a loudness that felt like the apocalypse was coming upon us; the car.

Then came a sharp whistling and the blast of a rocket; a missile, shooting past the alley entrance, and hitting home the machine gunner in a sound of shredding metal.

Like a divine miracle, the car stopped behind us, spinning it's rotary gun before unloading a storm of lead on the Reds before us, leaving the path dead.

We turned to face the monster car whose lights were blinding us.

"Holy shit, Dirk. You saved us!" I yelled out, but on clicked a speaker that proved me wrong about who was driving the car.

"Watch the cussin', Perc."

"Holden!?"

Out he stepped from the car, telling me how he came back to help, only to find the wheeled weapon abandoned, and couldn't help but finally take it for a spin. "-thought maybe we could use an extra hand." He told me, giving a '*come here*' gesture toward the car, and out stepped a man I almost didn't recognize, he looked bedraggled but fit.

"Heya, kid." He said, and I knew in an instant.

"Tyler."

"He'd gotten pinched by the cops soon after we did, but they sent him right to jail." Holden explained.

"Dude! You don't look too bad!" I said, punching him in the chest.

"Hah, yeah I sorta had to toughen up, but I guess same went for you and Hold, huh?" Tyler laughed.

"Yeah, man." I laughed back.

"Hey! Fellas, I like the reunion, real touching, but we've got a war to win!" The Commander reminded us.

"Yes, sir!" Holden and I said in unison, Tyler playing along with an exaggerated salute.

Doctor told us to arm Tyler, we salvaged a weapons and armor set from one of the fallen Reds.

Commander climbed behind the wheel, gathering us up before peeling out, circling the terminal, and bringing the fire of the remaining machine gunners upon us, the bullet barrage ceasing incrementally as Doctor missiled them into shrapnel.

Holden and Tyler then leaned out of the windows, taking shots at gathering soldiers in the area while Doctor ran over any in the streets. I took control of the rotary gun, clearing the scene in a blaze of gun-smoke.

I thought Doctor was preparing to exit the vehicle to raid the terminal, but instead he rammed us directly into the station, tearing through the building's glass and metal entrance, taking out a number of armed guards in the process.

"No more games." I heard him say to himself before calling us to action. "Boys, open fire!"

We all leapt out of the car, using the doors as barriers while combating an encirclement of encroaching opponents. Doctor shot a shotgun from one arm, and a full-auto from the other, dropping both in place of a canister-fed riot shotgun which he drove directly into the crowd without regard for the flying bullets. I reloaded the rotary gun, taking control of it, giving Tyler some supporting fire.

"Hold fire!" Doctor called out as the crowd dissolved in the span of a minute. We were the last lives in the entire grand hall. "Reload your guns. Holden, Tyler, I need both of you to man the car; if anyone so much as shows their face, wipe it off. Holiday, you're coming with me. There's no telling what's waiting for us down in that substation, so prepare for the worst."

We climbed into the elevator, clinging to opposite walls, guns readied toward the door.
We descended slowly down the elevator shaft, the mood was tense as the elevator hesitantly creaked it's way down. Out of nowhere, Doctor chuckled, smiling.

"What's so funny, sir?"

"*I found Rome a city of bricks, and I left it a city of marble.* Do you know who said that?"

"No, sir."

"Augustus Caesar." He smiled wider, looking at me before looking back to the door. "I used to see myself as the inheritor of a great legacy, the party of my commander, my country, left in chaos after his assassination, but I took it, and I made it greater than he could have ever imagined. I'm reminded of Caesar and Augustus." He looked back to me. "I almost forget the story doesn't end with them."

We were brought back to attention by the ding of the elevator bell as we reached the bottom level.

"No backing down." Doctor said with a nod. We scoped the scene before taking the ground, rifles up, leaving the sole man in the room in our sights. "Game's over, Nemo. Nowhere left to run, nowhere left to hide."

"Yes, I suppose so, Mr.Doctor." The man said with his hands raised, turning to face us slowly. "Perhaps I was too ambitious in my planning. I should have known a rematch in your very own city would end poorly, but to be fair, I believed you to be dead." He was too cocky for a man clearly at the end of his rope, he shrugged his shoulders nonchalantly. "But tell me, is so well versed a man, such as yourself, unfamiliar with mutually assured destruction?"

"What are you on about?" The Commander demanded.

"Look behind me; is grid system which indirectly joins every major city in North East. With modification, I've created killswitch which generates a pulse whose force will leave entire region in permanent blackout. Cities become cities no longer, industry collapses; best of all, this region contains highest concentration of nuclear reactors on entire continent. Without power, reactors will meltdown, destroying all you have built. If we cannot have the Megalopolis, neither will you. Countdown has already begun. I am prepared for death." I spied the man raising a gun to his head. I shot the weapon from his hand before he could do so. Doctor dashed forward, restraining him, pinning his head to the computer before us.

"Disable the countdown!" Doctor demanded.

"I have nothing to lose. I am already dead."

Doctor looked to the monitors, watching the counter countdown from ten minutes, he looked at me, and called out.

"Holiday! I have an idea! The car has a self-destruct function, the engine's nuclear, remove it, bring it down here; if there's any chance of stopping the countdown, it's by destroying this machine-" That moment, Nemo snapped back, swiping a gun from Doctor's side-holster to aim at me, Doctor knocked it from his hand, and the two were now locked in combat. "-GO! Do it now!" He called out.

I rushed into the elevator, taking it up, and quickly telling Holden the situation as we popped the hood, nervously but hastenly prying pieces surrounding the engine from the car until the spherical encasement labeled '*Nuclear*' was freed. Holden and I yanked out the small engine, leveraging its weight together, and carrying it into the elevator.

New York, Neu York
June 5 1981
|Mister Doctor|

The two of us struggled over my gun. For a man of his age, he carried a great deal of strength, fighting with the force of a crazed animal, but I ***was*** a crazed animal; I held nothing back against the man who'd murdered my commander before my eyes, who'd driven my home to collapse, and once again sought to tear down what I and my people rebuilt in the wake of his chaos.

I nearly drove his face through the floor. I broke the bones of his hand with my own. I savagely attempted to drive my arms through his torso until finally he lay bloodied and battered on the ground. I removed myself from him, sitting just a foot away.

I took in gasps of air like a hungry beast, looking at the timer drawing closer to its terminus.
Percy and Holden arrived, dropping the compact but heavy engine at my side.

"Thank you, boys. I'll take it from here, now go." I instructed them.

"Sir, there might not be enough time to-"

"I said **go**! This is what I must do." I assured Percy. Holden placed his hand on Percy's shoulder, insisting they leave, he begrudgingly did. "Holiday-!" I called out, he turned to face me. "-Remember your promise."

"Hail victory, sir."

"Hail victory." I responded as I watched the two of them ascend in the elevator, disappearing from my sight. The clock behind me was down to it's final minutes.
"Why'd you do it, Nemo?" I asked the man I knew was still conscious. "Why'd you do this to us?"

"Because men like you are murderers, monsters; you're savages who eat the most helpless of this world whenever you're given the chance. You are undeserving of power. ***You cannot handle power***!" He answered. I just smiled.

"Is that so?" I responded with a laugh. "I should've just shot you." I reflected on my missed opportunity. "I used to believe the best thing I could do to lead a peaceful, fruitful life, was to remove myself from situations, to simply ignore what others are doing, and let all be left alone to their own devices. I could have lived a very happy life as a farmer or fisher in Maine, I would have been happy to teach or work in a local business, maybe open my own someday. There was a time you could do that without needing to worry that your way of life was going to disappear, that your people might become the hated and oppressed in their own country." He watched me quietly through bloodied eyes. I continued. "You wouldn't understand that, now would you? Just having a place of your own to be content, no, you wanted this." I took in a deep breath. "The people changed, most apparently in the big cities where the popular culture dominated; the people changed because the culture suddenly changed, suddenly changed from disciplined, religious, moral, and unified to a plain unruly, arrogantly critical, hedonistic degeneracy. We were brought up by Hollywood and the education system to believe in aimless rebellion and false equality while our institutions of religion and racial identity were snatched away from us. We were a white nation, secular in government, but christian in character; we believed in fairness, in hard work, in serving something better than our individual selves, and suddenly it changed, changed from a home built for me, my people, to an all-welcoming whorehouse of a country. I blamed the communists, rightly. We'd entered a rivalry with the Soviets, and wanted to destroy each other, but I knew the sickness stretched deeper than the forties." I began priming the detonation sequence on the engine, knowing well the blast would be sufficient to fill the entire room, and collapse the structures above us. "I didn't always understand the Commander, how he would talk about the jews. I admit, at first I believed it a blind hatred, a scapegoat built on some misunderstanding, but I learned, I sought truth. I was very willing to listen and investigate, not for anyone but myself. You know what I found? The Rosenbergs, spies who gave Russia **OUR** bomb, starting this Cold War to begin with. Lev Bronstein, aka Leon Trotsky, head general of the Bolshevik revolution, dreamer of global revolution. Karl Liebneckt and Rosa Luxemberg, jewish leaders of the failed communist revolution in Germany, same of Bela Kun in Hungary, same of Blum in France. Lest we forget Karl Marx himself, and his early mentor Moses Hess, an advocate for both socialism and zionism. Now you, you are a jew, now aren't you? You come into my country, escaping the persecution of another, and you have the nerve to begin carving out of my own home a mansion for yourself, as several of your kind have done before not only here but abroad. I thought I could blame you alone for what has happened, but you were just one in a long line of trouble-makers, provocateurs, and manipulators. You owned our government, but who owned our culture? Hollywood, education, media. Who owns the three? Who owns our money? In a white country, should white men not control these facets of their home? No, you suppose not, after all, *we're undeserving of power*, just *dangerous savages* unfit to handle the very things we've built." I relaxed as I wrapped up what I wanted to say. "I've never been a man to wish harm upon another solely for his background, I've known many upstanding ethnics from Negros to Italians; some groups have a more difficult time cooperating with others, but more often then not, we all just want to be left alone to take care of ourselves; I used to think that was enough, but men like you, and your kind, are never content to leave us alone, and I understand why. I see why your people have been removed from Soviet Russia, you cannot defeat nature, you cannot change blood, you cannot control us like cattle. The fair man in me feels remorse for the innocent who are swept up because of the actions of a devious few, but the dismayed, logical man in me now knows extreme measures are the most effective ones, and I've made sure my successors don't repeat the merciful mistakes I have made." I activated the destruct countdown. "I truly do hate you." I said to him. He breathed tensely through his nose, sitting up, opposite me.

"I am not a monster." He finally said.

"Neither am I."

"Who are you to deny the world salvation?"

"I'm the protector of my people, and my people alone. I am Uncle Sam."

New York, Neu York
June 5 1981
|Percy Holiday|

Tyler was waiting for us on the surface, pushing the car toward the exit so we could still make use of it's weapons, but Holden advised him to just gather some supplies, and find a new vehicle off the street.

Tyler and I gathered some remaining ammunition, and two shotguns from the trunk. Holden called out to us a minute later, and pulled up in a run-down car he'd managed to hotwire to life off the street. Holden got out to help us load the supplies into our new escape vehicle, but within minutes, we heard a rumbling deep beneath our feet.

I hurried into the driver's seat, Tyler and Holden climbing in before we sped out just in time to escape the collapse of the station.

The harsh rumbling, and sinking of the building gave way to a stark silence.

Holden and I held our fists over our hearts, mourning Doctor. Tyler even paid his respects in that moment. Hours could have passed in the span of time we sat reflecting on this compounded sorrowful victory.

"I want to go home." I finally said, taking back the wheel of the car, and with Holden's nod of agreement, set course for Rockport.

I radioed my men to begin recapture of Red territory. Reinforcements were inbound.

The workaholic in me made sure to tie up loose ends, delegating command to my lieutenants or to commander Dirk if they reestablished contact with him.

It was now well past midnight. We'd driven for hours, mostly in silence. I hoped I could sleep this day away, sleep the whole mess away and put it in a bin of bad dreams.

For a minute I wondered what I would pay to be able to go back to the way things were when everything was simple. That was foolish in hindsight, we can't choose the hand life deals us, we just do the best we can with it; I just felt drained, like I needed a vacation.

No one said this was going to be easy, hell I've been told the opposite consistently, so I guess this *is* what I signed up for, these are the cards I was dealt. Dealt a heavy responsibility, I was, and truth be told, it scared me, but the way I saw it, I've got a problem that if I outrun, everyone else is going to have to deal with; kids growing up right now like I did, repeating this damn cycle of hopelessness. No, I'm going to face this, and I'm going to put it in the grave for as long as I'm alive, so no one else has to.

When I'm gone, I'd hope I set enough of an example for the next guy to do just as good as I did, if not better. That cheered me up, dispelled my fear, and replaced it with hope, an ambition to make sure I don't let Doctor down.

"We're here, Percy." Tyler said, knocking on his window.

I pulled into a space in front of his place, a townhouse he'd been renting, and where we'd be spending our nights until we got readjusted.

New England Commonwealth, Rockport Town
June 6 1981
|Percy Holiday|

Holden prepped some breakfast for the three of us. Tyler was watching some television. I was just coming down the stairs. The world felt strangely alive, it was a good feeling, difficult to describe, but I felt in my gut an optimism I hadn't felt in a long time. I must've smiled my biggest smile of the year.
"*It's good to be back.*" I thought.

I got myself ready for the day, dressing down the uniform by rolling up the shirt sleeves, and leaving the jacket on it's hanger. I joined the boys for breakfast and some morning entertainment.

Out of nowhere we got a knock at the door, and I realized I'd been expecting this more than I even knew. I answered the door to be greeted by a pair of men who addressed me as '*Commander Holiday*'. The men informed me that Doctor left to me a letter, and that I was needed to report to Kingston Base Camp to begin overseeing the commonwealth. I assured them I'd be there in due time, and excused myself back into the house.

"What's the word, Perc?" Holden asked.

"Duty calls, it looks like." I opened the letter, finding a key, and a paper that read '*Don't let me down*' followed by an address.

"Now what do you make of that, Perc?" Holden asked, leaning in to read. "That's uh-, that's in Maine, there. We must've passed that address some point on our trip, I bet. You boys up for another trip? I sure as hell am." Holden clapped his hands together gleefully. Tyler affirmed his interest in a get-away after these last few years. They were excited to see where this would lead us, I admit, I was as well.

Tyler'd had his old car set up in a garage, still as beautiful as I remembered.

"Now it ain't nuclear, but it'll get the job done." Tyler joked.

We climbed in, Holden grasping the leather of the seat as if savoring a flavor from his childhood. Tyler's cassette from that night we were picked up was still in the player, continuing the last song we left off on. We were all a bit shaken by the tune, but not necessarily in a negative sense, more like, how it felt so well preserved, this feeling we felt, that is, like it'd been saved in a box, waiting for us to return, now here we are, as if it never happened.

Tyler looked to Holden, who in turn looked to me, and I back at Tyler. I knew what we were all thinking: *Drive, drive away, forget all this ever happened*; the temptation was strong.

"We'll make one stop along the way-" Holden said. "-Old Orchard Beach, where we went last time. We'll get some sodas, maybe a beer, just take in a little bit of sun, then we take off."

I gave him a nod, and so we did.

After hours on the road, wind blowing through our hair, music playing, forests and drive-thru towns passing us by all along the road, we finally reached our first stop.

The sun was shining bright, people were laughing and smiling like they always do. It was just how I imagined.

We took in the place, barely speaking a word the whole time there, just relishing this moment we'd been dreaming about for two years now, and it was absolutely worth it.

Now there was something new for me to set out on, a new dream, a new vision to make a reality, and it began at our last stop which brought us to an old, overgrown, abandoned fort just north of Portland and south of Augusta.

I wasn't really sure what I was looking for, I just had this key and the address. We wandered the site looking for a chest, or a door, something that would need to be opened, and that's when I found something that stood out; I saw an etching of what looked to be a Roman, the image was my height, and between the bricks was empty space, as if they'd never been cemented.

Just out of curiosity, I pulled at one of the bricks, loosening it enough to grind it out; behind it laid more loose bricks which I more eagerly began removing until finally, I uncovered a worn, wooden panel door, a faded swastika painted atop it, and a lock which fit my key, granting me access to the vault which was so dark I couldn't see a foot ahead of me.

"Need a light?" Holden asked, passing me a lighter. I stumbled on a candle lamp which helped me to more clearly see the room around me; I was in awe.

"Holden! Tyler! You're gonna wanna see this! Bring a flashlight or something if you've got one!"

The two came running, gawking at the sight of some two dozen silver ingots, labeled at about eight pounds each. We found by the ingots a number of weapons mounted to the wall, and a set of books in protective storage atop a desk. On the desk was what appeared to be a recently wrapped package, upon opening it, I found a pair of new, red, pinstripe pants, and a navy-blue vest; between them was another letter, a letter addressed from Commander Doctor.

Chapter 9

Gran California, Commonwealth Council at Culver City
September 7 1981
|Doc Tiberius Holiday|

Very busy day, a lot of hands to shake, and a long speech to make. I was happy the good men in the California Government were able to accommodate both transportation and hosting of the event. The California President was very happy to have myself and the other presidents as honored guests for the first meeting of the Reunited States Council, as it was known here. I prefer Doctor's title of the Commonwealth Council, but they were all just regional interchangeable names for the same thing.

I enjoyed meeting personally with presidents Houston and Smith of Texas and Deseret respectively. Houston gave his condolences for the loss of Doctor, assuring me I'd have his personal support in any matter. Houston asked me of Dirk, what had become of him, I wish I could say. We scoured the streets for him, for a body even, but not a trace was found, he seemingly vanished in the chaos. We also tried to locate what remained of Bull, but again, no luck. Maybe they both walked away that day, each managing to go back to something better back home; perhaps the two killed one another, or some combination of the two.

President Smith too welcomed me, as the youngest of the leaders, with open arms, formally introducing me to president Davis of Dixie.

Us four were something of a cohesive bloc, we had stuck together the longest, and understood how the system worked. Davis and I extended an olive branch to President Long of Great Louisiana, a fence-sitter whose policies grossly contrasted from ours, but we reassured him of our stance on self-determination.

We got to know well the leaders of the reorganized commonwealths, the lands that were at one point occupied territories: Heartland, Cascadia, Superior, and Ford; their presidents came from the backgrounds of a farmer, a woodsman, a businessman, and an engineer respectively, they, like me, were something of an oddball, only recently taking office, but unlike me, lacking the connections Doctor had passed on to my administration; I thus took it upon myself to welcome them, introduce them to our brothers, and bring them up to speed on the event.

This was a conference to officially announce the total reunification of all former states into the Confederation of New Amerika.
Finally our power would be whole again. We'd continue to enjoy the fruits of self-determination within our own homes, occupied by our own people, who lived our shared lifestyles, while providing for our

brotherlands the resources they need, as they do for us in a mutualist harmony.

Most of us had ethnic self-determination enshrined in our commonwealth constitutions, New England, Dixie, Deseret, and Texas all upheld separation of demographic minority communities to limited areas, and encouraged most to move elsewhere through paid repatriation, or other means. Keeping our demographics secure was key to further ensure future generations would follow in our footsteps.

We all had different values, laws we wanted to preserve and uphold in our commonwealth communities; our individual constitutions provided a base document for how each of us would go about conducting ourselves in our own distinct ways, while the federal constitution, or *United Constitution* as some preferred to call it, laid out the shared foundations of our commonwealths as successors to the original states, and as a united family of Amerikan lands; it ensured no one commonwealth would impose it's will over another, ensured we'd stand together in the name of defense, it prevented any single commonwealth from developing independent international relations, and enshrined the core importances of self sovereignty, and remaining a homogenous, united people within each of our respective lands. Gran California, and Great Louisiana took a more liberal approach to this order in the form of Civic Nationalism, identity through ideology alone. We left it as the job of time to judge the wiseness of their decision, and did not interfere with their choices. The rest of us, on the other hand, decided to codify more strict definitions of what it meant to be one of us.

Internationally we began to recede from the realm of politics; we strived for self-sufficiency, and made no obligations to any foreign state, nor formed any dependencies.

In the absence of the internationalist American hegemony, the Soviets had conquered the vastness of Asia, leaving only fragments of Arabia free of Communist rule.
Japan, and the Philippines sought security from the remaining Western Superpowers of Great Britain and France.

Not many knew of the strained relationship between Doctor and Bull outside of the Confederation, overseas the two were idolized, most especially Bull, triggering a similar political shift in Britain, driving them to take Japan, and the Philippines under their protection in exchange for resources, port access, and special privileges for Anglo citizens within both nations. The increased need to reach the two island nations more quickly led to greater cooperation with the South African government, reintroducing it into the Commonwealth of Nations. The ***CoN*** itself would bring closer it's bonds, specifically between the UK, Australia, South Africa, New Zealand, and Canada to better secure one another against Soviet aggression, this alliance had come to be known as the Imperial Union, and function with England as it's head, reviving the empire as Bull had always wanted.

Communism had seemingly been contained to Asia and small pockets across the other continents. On our front, Dixie did an upstanding and consistent job of beating back the Cubans.

It started to seem like the world didn't need us, and thankfully so. It's more than about time we started focusing on us again.

We'd gathered together in the big meeting hall, sitting in front of our respective Commonwealth flags, as a crowd of several thousand eagerly waited on us to speak.

"This is a momentous occasion-" I started. "-I know when I took office, there was a great deal of controversy. I didn't understand it myself when Doctor first told me I was to be his successor. Certainly I felt I'd done well in the army, but I knew of men far more skilled than myself; majors and captains who led the securing of Washington

D.C, protected the boroughs of New York long before I ever set foot on the land, and led men in far greater number than I ever had. I now know he chose me because he knew of no other man who had shared his virtues and experiences quite like myself, and he believed that I would do in his place exactly what he himself set out to achieve. I do my best everyday to ensure that I honor his legacy, and do the very best for us all, as he would have wanted." They once again clapped, and cheered me on.

"Our homes belong not only to us, but to our offspring; future generations who, as nature intended, succeed us, carrying forward and refining who we are into ever improving forms." I took a pause, thinking back.

"So often in our generation, and in recent past generations, we've seen an objection of this rule of nature, of offspring increasingly rejecting the teachings their parents spent a lifetime acquiring, in favor of a poisonous rebellion identity imposed by the enemies of tradition, an identity whose only purpose is to destroy that of others, dropping these poor, misguided souls into spiraling decadence and self destruction. Today, in the Confederation of New Amerika, we say ***Never Again***! Our children are us, and we are them. If only men like us could build a society like our own, then only our children can continue to maintain and improve it for our people. This is a simple, yet critical truth to the survival of any civilization, one which should be ingrained into the very fabric of government, and that is precisely what we in this New Order will achieve! A land for all our peoples, free and independent, strong and united."

The audience cheered, my fellow presidents presented their speeches, and addressed other orders of business regarding commonwealth rights, personal rights, travel between commonwealths, et cetera, before we began taking questions for the press; one happened to have a question for me specifically.

"As you said, there's been a good deal of controversy surrounding you, particularly about your age, inexperience, and really who you are. Frankly you seem to be something of a dark horse, you weren't particularly high ranking, or remarkable, at least as far as public record shows. It's all well and good that you believe you and Commander Doctor saw eye to eye, but what proves to us that you're fit to serve as the President of New England?"

I took a moment to consider his question before I answered.

"Had I believed common convention, I would have agreed with you. Doctor was a rather fond historian; he himself believed I would be best fit for this position even when I myself didn't. I sought to studying precedence for young leaders: Karl of Sweden, taking throne at fifteen, and dominating the empires of Poland and Russia in the Great Northern War. Alexander the Great who ascended the throne at twenty to go on and conquer the known world. Marquis de Lafayette who became a major general in our very first revolution at age nineteen. There's a certain something about youth, a fiery passion in these early years that moves us to take monumental action, and really strive for change. A passion that leads boys to take up arms for what they believe in, regardless of cost to self, though so often our eagerness to act is exploited by those willing to harvest this fire of youth. We, young men, are the burning engines that propel society forward. Our only downfall is our naivety, and inexperience."

He had his criticism prepared.

"Yes, and on the matter of inexperience, you don't seem to be very experienced yourself."

"I'd hoped my actions spoke more loudly than the criticisms of my character. It's true I'm not a politician, but I know what makes New England, *New England*. I know what our problems are, I know what my people want to do about these problems, and I've foregone the lazy bureaucracy to just do what needs to be done." There was a momentary silence before I continued. "As of far, I've brought steady progress to New England, this leadership will not be without it's falls and mistakes, but I know well to not only learn from my mistakes, but to learn quickly. Yes, there was a time I was so inexperienced that I hardly knew who I was or even where I was going, for many of you, this is unfortunately your reality even late into life; I learned the cost and value of sacrifice and life personally under Major General Del Kirk. I learned the importance of blood and sweat from my missions with Captain Fuse. I learned the value of fierce, precise, and unrestrained action through my observation of Captain Johnny Bull. I learned more than I could ever imagine from the words, writing, and actions of Commander Augustus Doctor. I'm not a naive child whose merely read the achievements of great men, I'm a soldier whose stood shoulder to shoulder with former leaders of this land, I'm a man who rose from a life of poverty and hardship to earn the title of President by physically fighting for the rights of my people, and the security of our way of life. I'm Amerika, and Amerika is me. I am Uncle Sam."

I Am Uncle Sam

Made in the USA
Monee, IL
25 November 2019

17456848R00118